Finding Nick

JANIS REAMS HUDSON

MILLS & BOON™

Pure reading pleasure

First published in Great Britain 2007
Large Print edition 2007
Silhouette Books Limited, Eton House,
18-24 Paradise Road, Richmond, Surrey, TW9 1SR

© Janis Reams Hudson 2006

ISBN-13: 978 0 263 19881 2

Set in Times Roman 18 on 23 pt.
35-1107-49443

Printed and bound in Great Britain
by Antony Rowe Ltd, Chippenham, Wiltshire

JANIS REAMS HUDSON

was born in California, grew up in Colorado, lived in Texas for a few years and now calls central Oklahoma home. She is the author of more than twenty-five novels, both contemporary and historical romances. Her books have appeared on the Waldenbooks, B. Dalton and BookRak bestseller lists and earned numerous awards, including the National Reader's Choice Award and Reviewer's Choice awards from *Romantic Times BOOKclub*. She is a three-time finalist for the coveted RITA® Award from Romance Writers of America and is a past president of RWA.

This book is dedicated with gratitude and awe to firefighters everywhere. Please stay safe!

Prologue

The dream came again, as it did most nights. Never let it be said that Nick Carlucci made it through a week without the horror of it. The blinding, choking dust and ash. The flames. Rubble so hot that it melts the soles of your boots.

The frantic search for survivors. Any survivors, but especially his father and brother, please God.

Then the moan, the hand that moves.

Frantic digging. *Hold on! I've got you, man.*

Spirits soar. Breath rasps. Dig faster!

Then he has him. The man speaks.

Elation!

A minute later, the stranger dies in Nick's arms.

He tries to hang on to the man's lifeless body, but others take it from him.

Failure. He'd failed to save that man.

Search more. Dig more. Shout. Maybe someone can hear.

Then the beam, still smoking from the inferno, twisted now into a grotesque shape. It sways.

Look out!

They don't hear him, the men standing in the path of the deadly steel. With arms outstretched, he leaps, knocking the men out of harm's way.

Pain! Screaming, white-hot pain in his back.

Then…nothing.

Nick woke gasping for air, his bed a pool of sweat. It was the same every time the nightmare came to torment him. He rubbed the ache in his hip and thigh, and fought to push the memories away.

But the memories stayed. They always did. So did the pain. The sense of failure, of uselessness.

The guilt.

Could he have dug deeper, faster? Had he missed someone?

I should have been inside. I should have died with the others. With Pop and Vinnie.

He fought his way out of the damp, tangled sheet. There would be no more sleep for him this night. Jim Beam would keep him company. Whiskey helped him forget, for a little while, that life, as he'd known it, was forever gone.

Chapter One

Autumn 2006
Tribute, Texas

He'd been hailed a hero on the streets of New York, on worldwide television, even at his old firehouse, Rescue Company One, but Nick Carlucci knew better. He was nothing more than a washed-up failure. A has-been who never was.

Some hero, he thought with a derisive snort, when something as simple as the sky could make the hair on the back of his neck stand on end.

It wasn't the sky, exactly, he admitted. It was that there was so damn much of it here in the small Texas town of Tribute. He'd been in town more than two years now, and he still wasn't used to so much emptiness overhead. Or so much quiet. Or so much fresh air. Or so little traffic, so few people.

He was used to skyscrapers, traffic jams, exhaust fumes. Crowds of people. Subways. Elevators. Taxicabs.

He was used to home. New York.

In Tribute, Texas, there wasn't a single taxicab to be had, much less a subway, unless he counted the gopher tunnels that crisscrossed his aunt's backyard. Subway for rodents.

A traffic jam in Tribute was more than three cars backed up at the one and only traffic light on Main Street.

As for skyscrapers, the tallest man-made structure for thirty miles in any direction was the grain silo over by the railroad tracks.

How had he come to like it here? He shook his head. Who would have thought? He had wanted a way out of the mess his life had become, and he'd ended up here, halfway across the country, in Texas.

Not that Nick's ego was so big that he thought for a minute that his uncle Gil had died two years ago simply so Nick would be needed in Dallas to help Aunt Bev settle her husband's estate and move back to Tribute, where she'd lived years ago.

No, Nick wasn't taking the rap for that one. Gil had been on a first-name basis with leukemia for years. His death had nothing to do with Nick's needs.

What Nick needed now was a restored sex drive, and a woman to go with it.

He reached Main Street and paused on the curb while a car crawled by. The driver honked and waved. Not a typical New York one-finger wave, but a friendly wave for Bev Watson's nephew. The local high-school janitor.

Wasn't that a kick in the butt. From putting out fires, saving property and lives, to mopping floors. Some would call that a serious comedown. Nick didn't look at it that way. He was learning that there was something incredibly satisfying in turning a dull, dirty floor into a spotless, gleaming surface.

He nearly laughed out loud at the thought. He was becoming a 1950s housewife. Move over, June Cleaver.

Nick returned the driver's wave, not because he felt particularly friendly, but because that's what people did around here. Besides, he thought that might be the mayor's cousin, who was a friend of Aunt Bev's. No use being rude and having Bev catch the flack for it merely because Nick was feeling surly. Surly was nothing knew for him these days. It was more like his natural state. Besides, it was Monday.

With no more cars coming, Nick crossed the street, careful to step down from the curb with his good leg, in case his bad one decided to lock up on him and send him sprawling face-first to the ground.

Oh, yeah. The big, tough hero.

Three more blocks brought him to the high school, home of the Tribute Tigers. As he walked up the sidewalk to the main entrance, he unclipped the wad of keys from his belt and felt his surly mood slip away.

He liked this school. He liked the kids, the staff, his job. He felt useful here, like a productive member of society again.

It beat the hell out of drinking all day, and this way, he could look himself in the mirror without sneering.

Inside the quiet building, he took his usual walk down the length of the entire hall and back, listening to the sound of his steps echo in the emptiness.

It wouldn't be empty long. Soon hundreds of feet would join his on these floors. It was time to get to work.

Sitting in her rental car across the street from Tribute High, Shannon Malloy watched the man unlock the school door and felt her pulse leap. It was him. There was no mistake. Nicholas Giovanni Carlucci, in the flesh. And my, oh my, what flesh it was, she thought with a grin. The file photos from the newspapers and the video footage from television had not done the man justice, but those jeans he was wearing today certainly did.

He was tall, maybe an inch or two over six feet, with broad shoulders and lean hips. His hair was shiny black; his eyes, in the photos, were Italian dark, although she had yet to verify that.

If she hadn't known for a fact that he had suffered a broken back and crushed pelvis and thigh, she might not have noticed the slight limp as he had made his way across the street and up the sidewalk to the big double glass doors. After all, the doctors had said he would never walk again. Nick Carlucci was a living, breathing testament to a will of steel—every bit as hard and strong as the giant steel I beam that had nearly killed him.

Never walk again? He walked just fine. She'd spotted the slight hitch in his gait only because she had followed the line of his jeans down to his cowboy boots.

It was all Shannon could do to keep from leaping out of the car and rushing into the school to catch up with him.

The impulse startled her. Not that she wasn't impulsive by nature, because she'd been known to be. But she was also a professional journalist who knew when to push—or in this case, rush—and when to bide her time.

She'd been gnashing her teeth for weeks trying to get an interview with Carlucci, but he had refused to return her calls. She had finally tracked him down and followed him across the country. To hell with biding her time. She had him in her sights and wasn't about to let him slip away. Now, before anyone else showed up, was probably her best chance to talk to him.

Shannon made her move. She slipped from her car and hustled up the sidewalk and into the school.

She wasn't sure why her heart was pounding as she stood in the silent building that was empty save for her and her quarry. This was just another interview, and she had done so many that she couldn't count them all. But as she stood at the end of the hall and watched Nick Carlucci walk toward her, she somehow knew that this interview, this subject, this man, would be different.

Slight limp aside, it took no time at all for those long legs of his to eat up the distance between them. As he neared, he slowed and cocked his head. "May I help you?"

Shannon held out her hand. "Mr. Carlucci, I'm—"

That was as far as she got because the instant his hand touched hers, every thought, every scrap of sense—including her own name—flew right out of her head. She couldn't speak, couldn't think. Could only feel as heated sensation zapped through her, shooting from head to toe, emanating from where his hand touched hers.

Palm to palm, flesh to flesh, they stared at each other, eyes—his and hers—wide with shock.

Tingling heat settled low and deep in her belly. A vivid picture of this man rising over her in bed made her gasp. With tremendous effort, she pulled her hand from his. The sharp, sexual sensation lessened, but did not completely abate.

"Wow." A slow, puzzled smile spread across Nick Carlucci's face. Those dark eyes told her he had felt the same startling charge of electricity that she had.

For a woman who made her living with words, Shannon found herself in the unusual position of having none. She was saved from stammering or babbling like a fool—or jumping his bones right there in the hall of the school—by the banging of a door somewhere down the hall.

Shannon blinked. She would have left just then—she was that shaken by her reaction to this man, but as she stepped back he managed to snare her arm.

"Hold on," he said. "I didn't catch your name."

Through sheer effort Shannon managed to gather a few of her wits and remember what she was supposed to be doing here. "Shannon Malloy," she said.

The smile on his face slowly faded. "You're kidding."

"No."

"No." His voice turned grim; he released her arm. "You wouldn't be, would you?"

"Wouldn't be?"

"Kidding."

"No." She shook her head.

He swore. "You followed me across half a damn country?"

It was difficult, considering lust still fogged her brain, but she managed a shrug. "You wouldn't return my calls."

"So you *followed* me?"

She shrugged again.

"Did it ever occur to you that I didn't return your calls because I didn't want to talk to you?"

She couldn't do this, Shannon thought. She couldn't push or cajole him into an interview when she was still so off balance from this unreasonably fierce attraction that still gripped her.

"Look," she said, struggling to keep her voice even. "I know this is a bad time. I've caught you by surprise at your job." She took a step backward. "I'll be in touch later to set up a time that's more convenient for you."

And she fled. For the first time in her life, she fled from a man, from an interview subject. From herself.

Nick stood in the hall and watched her go. He could have stopped her. Part of him wanted to. But the smart part ruled. He turned away and shook his head.

It just went to prove what a sense of humor Fate had. Only minutes earlier Nick had been wanting a restored sex drive, and a woman to go with it. And he'd gotten both, in spades. Never had he experienced a reaction like that from a mere handshake. The sheer irony that of all the women in the world, it was Shannon Malloy who sparked that reaction in him had him grinding his teeth and biting back a curse.

A damn *reporter,* he thought with disgust.

She must be part bloodhound because Nick knew he wasn't all that easy to find. Unless…no, surely Bev wouldn't…. Then again, reporters, he knew from past experience, could be tricky. The good ones could get information out of a rock if they wanted it badly enough.

This particular reporter had ferreted out his phone number a few weeks ago and started leaving him messages. She was doing a book on 9/11 rescue workers and wanted to interview him.

He couldn't imagine who would want to read a book about that five years after the fact, but she must have conned some publisher into it or she wouldn't have come all the way to Texas to see him.

Well, he thought as he crossed to the supply closet to get a replacement for the fluorescent light flickering at the other end of the hall, Shannon Malloy had wasted her time and money tracking him down because he didn't have a damn thing to say. As far as he was concerned, all reporters belonged at the bottom of the East River, with heavy concrete slabs tied to their ankles to keep them there.

From now on he was going to find out who a woman was *before* he shook hands with her and went blind with lust.

In his defense, when the doctors had told him five years ago that he would never walk again, *walk* had been a polite euphemism for *feel or do or control anything below the waist.* It was surely only bad luck and worse timing that Shannon Malloy happened to be the nearest woman around when his libido decided to come back to life.

Shannon made it back to her motel room at the Tribute Inn in less than five minutes. The way her heart was racing, it was a wonder she hadn't hit something with her car on the way.

Her hand still tingled from Nick Carlucci's touch. She took a deep breath and thought seriously about never washing that hand again.

Then she burst out laughing and fell back onto the bed. She couldn't believe how stupid she'd been! She'd had Nick Carlucci right there and had fled like a scared rabbit.

So why was she laughing?

Maybe she needed therapy, she thought. Because she was laughing in sheer anticipation of seeing Nick Carlucci again.

Of course, she had to see him again. Her book would not be complete without a section on him. She knew that; half of New York knew that, which was why she'd gone to the trouble of tracking him down. And he hadn't been an easy man to find, either.

But she'd kept at it until she'd found him because so many of the other people she'd interviewed for her book had told her it wouldn't be complete without at least a chapter on the man who had put himself in harm's way and taken a crippling blow to save the lives of seven others.

Several of the firefighters who had expressed that opinion also wondered where he'd gone, what had happened to him. Apparently when Nick Carlucci had left New York more than two years ago, he had severed all ties; none of his former buddies had known where he was. Perhaps because none of them possessed Shannon's tenacity. For the book to honor her father, it had to be the best. If that meant including Carlucci, she *would* find him.

She'd dug around on the Internet and learned that he had an aunt in Dallas. The aunt's husband had died right about the same time Carlucci had left New York. Shannon's instincts told her that his departure was not a coincidence.

While she'd found no sign of her quarry in

Dallas, she had tracked the aunt back to her childhood hometown, Tribute. It was there—here—where signs of Carlucci's presence had popped up.

Shannon was so busy patting herself on the back for finding him that she nearly missed the low vibration coming from her purse. When she finally heard it, she sat up and grabbed her cell phone from the bag.

"Hey, Mama," she said when she answered.

"Where are you, hon? You were supposed to call me last night."

"Sorry. I got into Dallas after midnight. I didn't think you'd want me to call that late."

Her mother chuckled. "I'm not sure which would have been worse—lying awake worrying about you, or hearing the phone ring in the middle of the night, which usually means bad news."

Shannon stood and paced the length of the room and back while she talked. "I was hoping you'd give me some credit and concede that I'm an adult and that I'm capable of getting on a plane and checking into a motel without calling my mommy."

"I hope you were smiling when you said that, young lady."

Shannon laughed. "I give up. I'm sorry I didn't call you last night. Forgive me?"

"All right, yes. Did you find that man you needed to interview?"

"I did, for all the good it did me," she confessed.

"He wouldn't talk?" her mother asked.

"No, but I haven't finished with him." In more ways than one, Shannon thought.

"I would hope not. It wouldn't be like you to go after a story and not get one."

"Oh, I'll get a story out of him. Nick Carlucci," she vowed, "has met his match."

The man in question spent his day as he did every weekday, maintaining the Tribute High School buildings and grounds. He changed the flickering lightbulb he'd found first thing that morning before that Malloy woman had found him.

Just how the heck had she done that, anyway? Who could have ratted him out?

Wade Harrison. If that son of a—

No, Wade wouldn't have told anyone how to find Nick. Would he?

Nick shook his head at the idea. If a story on the whereabouts of Nick Carlucci was such a hot idea, Wade would have done one himself and gotten the scoop on all the big-city papers and tabloids with his small-town weekly *Tribute Banner.* True, Harrison was the only one in town other than Nick's aunt, a couple of school board members and the high-school principal who knew about Nick's past, but it didn't make sense that the man would give him away after swearing not to.

Nick hadn't given *him* away when he'd come to town last summer and no one had realized who he was. Nick had recognized him, but Nick was from New York, as was Wade. In New York hardly a day went by that one paper or the other hadn't had a story about Wade Harrison, President and CEO of Harrison Corporation, one of the largest media conglomerates in the country.

Wade had come to town last summer for personal reasons, and Nick had kept his secret.

Of course, Wade's presence was now common knowledge since his marriage to

Dixie McCormick last month. The population of Tribute must have doubled during the week that the media had descended like a plague of locusts.

But prior to that, no one in town had realized who Wade was. No one but Nick, and he'd kept his mouth shut.

No, he didn't think Wade had given him away. This Malloy woman must be some kind of bloodhound.

So she'd found him. Big deal. That didn't mean he had to talk to her. She had let him off easy this morning, but he didn't think she had come all this way to give up after one try.

Let her try again, he thought. He had nothing to say.

Throughout the rest of the morning, as he replaced a light switch in the boys' locker room and unclogged a drain in the girls' shower, he kept expecting the woman to show up again. You'd think she'd have gotten the message that he didn't want to talk to her when he'd failed to return any of her numerous phone calls over the past few weeks.

But had she taken the hint? No, not Lois Lane. She had to show up and get in his face.

Why the *hell* did *she* have to be the first woman he responded to in years?

At least he knew now that all his parts worked. Except his hip now and then, but who was counting? It was only a hip. Just because it prevented him from fighting fires and saving lives, that didn't mean he couldn't still mop floors and change light-bulbs for a living.

If his thoughts were tinged with bitterness, Nick figured he was entitled.

But he really did like his current job. What

he had yet to learn was how to handle other people's opinions of what he did for a living.

"You're a *janitor?*" Said with a slight curl of the lip.

"You mop floors?" Said with a look of expectancy, like *Okay, so tell me the important part of your job.*

No matter what was said or asked, what was meant was "When are you going to get a *real* job?" or "meaningful work?"

Nick swore that the next time somebody asked that, he was going to invite them to come in and clean up the next time one of the kids came to school with a cold or flu and hurled all over the bathroom floor. *Clean that up and tell me it's not work, bub.*

Nick grimaced and shot a look over his shoulder to make sure no one was around, in case he'd been talking out loud to himself.

To his relief, he was alone in the short hall to the science lab. There was no class in the lab that period. Nick used the time to make his daily check on the five-foot-long rat snake, which had gotten a little too clever at getting out of his aquarium lately.

"Methinks you've been getting a little help, hey, Sir Rodney? At least you don't have some pesky reporter after you, wanting you to spill your guts because *the public has a right to know.* Don't you believe it, pal." He dropped some protein pellets into Rodney's glass tank—to tide him over until his next serving of rodent sushi. "All you gotta do is keep your mouth shut. If you don't talk, they can't misquote you. Of course, then they might put words in your mouth, but there's not much a man—sorry, a snake—can do about that."

That was the problem with reporters, Nick

acknowledged as he let himself out of the science lab. If they couldn't get you one way, they'd get you another. Given his choice, he figured he'd let Lois Lane make up whatever she wanted because he wasn't spilling his guts for anybody.

On his way down the hall he glanced over his shoulder, not for the first time that day. He told himself he wasn't looking for Shannon Malloy. He was just making sure she didn't sneak up on him. She was bound to come at him again.

Remembering the sharp electric charge that had zipped up his arm and settled in his groin that morning, he had to admit that he wouldn't mind shaking her hand again.

But he wasn't going to submit to an interview. If she pushed, he would push back. Shannon Malloy had met her match.

Chapter Two

On Tuesday, Shannon regrouped and readied herself to take another run at Nick Carlucci. This time she would wait until he got off work. Assuming he got off about the time school let out, she slept in—clear till nine— and felt like a woman of leisure. Or the lazy bum she'd never had a chance to be.

After a lengthy shower, she set out on foot

to explore the thriving metropolis of Tribute, Texas, population 2,793. Her first stop, about four blocks down Main from her motel, was a place called Dixie's Diner. The smell of bacon drew her inside.

As she entered and took a booth along the far wall, she wondered if the place took its name from a person, or from the fact that it was located in the South. Her answer came a moment later when her waitress brought her a tall tumbler of ice water and a menu. The waitress's name, according to the red-and-white plastic tag pinned above her right breast, was Dixie. Mystery solved.

After a breakfast guaranteed to test the strength of the button on her slacks, Shannon set out to see the rest of the town.

It didn't take all day, of course. The town just wasn't that large. But she took her time and visited several shops, the library, a couple of gift shops. In one, she found a small watercolor of Texas bluebonnets by a local artist; her mother would love it.

Across the square from the gift shop, Shannon spotted the offices of the *Tribute Banner.* Her heart skipped a beat. Every reporter worth her salt—most of the country, for that matter—knew that Wade Harrison, the country's wealthiest, most eligible bachelor, former president and CEO of Harrison Corporation, which was one of the nation's largest media giants, had left New York and corporate America last summer to edit and publish the *Tribute Banner* in Small Town, Texas.

The news and entertainment industries were still reeling. Harrison had been out of the corporate picture much of the past two years due to a heart transplant, but he'd been on his way back into the limelight when *poof*. He had dropped off the radar, then re-appeared weeks later to announce not only his purchase of the local weekly newspaper, but also his marriage to a woman from this very town. McCormick, or something like that, Shannon remembered.

"Holy moley." Shannon stopped in her tracks on the sidewalk. She stared at the newspaper office, then back at the diner where she'd eaten breakfast. Dixie's Diner. Dixie, the waitress who'd served her. Dixie McCormick. "Dixie McCormick Harrison, for crying out loud."

The woman rose another notch in Shannon's eyes. Not because she'd snagged one of the richest men in the country, but because she owned her own business and was sticking with it when she no longer needed to earn a living. Dixie was a woman worth admiring.

Shannon walked back to her motel and spent the remaining time until school let out editing and polishing the first part of her manuscript. By the time she came up for air, she had to rush to get over to the school before classes let out for the day.

She had wanted to walk, but there was no time now, so she drove. She parked across the street again, as she had the day before, and waited. From the corner of her eye she could see the school parking lot.

Less than five minutes later, a bell rang and teenagers erupted from the building. There was something odd about them. It took her a minute to realize that every other person coming out of the school, be it a boy, girl or adult, was wearing…bib overalls? What the…

Shannon shook her head and looked again. No mistake. At least half of the people leaving the school had on overalls. She didn't recall ever seeing someone wear them before, outside of a TV show or movie.

And straw hats. Some western, some more like something you'd expect to find on Tom Sawyer. Or Ellie May Clampett.

Man alive, she knew Tribute was a small town, but this was ridiculous.

She shook her head again and focused her attention on looking for Carlucci. Maybe she would ask him, use the overalls as an icebreaker.

And there he was, sauntering out the door with a group of boys, all of them—including Carlucci—wearing the ubiquitous bib overalls. She got out of her car and crossed the street, where she stood at the end of the sidewalk and waited for him.

Bib overalls, for crying out loud, and the mere sight of the man still made her heart race.

This could not be happening to her.

Nick saw her there—the frowning reporter—and drew to a halt. She had lulled him into a false sense of security by not coming back yesterday. He'd thought—hoped—he'd been free of her.

No such luck.

"Who's the babe?" Ricky Cooledge asked.

"The what?" Nick finally pulled his gaze from Malloy and looked at Cooledge.

"The one you've obviously got the hots for."

I don't have the hots for her. Much. Really.

"Who is she?" Tim Dean asked.

"Where's she from?" Ricky wanted to know.

"Hey, lady," Boss Bosco yelled. "You here to see Nick?"

"Gentlemen," Nick said, a quiet warning in his voice, "remember your manners."

"Yessir." All three boys saluted, but their grins said, *Manners? Yeah, right. Wait'll your back's turned, buddy.*

Before Nick's eyes, Malloy lost her frown and smiled brightly, with an odd gleam in her eyes as if she were mentally rubbing her palms together in anticipation of something he was sure he wouldn't like.

"Speaking of manners, Nick," she said, "are you going to introduce me to your friends?" *Try to avoid me now, pal, I dare you,* her expression seemed to say.

Trapped by his own words, Nick introduced her to the three teenagers. He watched carefully as she shook hands with each of them. The boys nearly fell all over themselves showing off for her, but Nick couldn't detect anything approaching the type of reaction in them that he'd had to shaking her hand yesterday.

"They'd love to hang around and talk," he announced, "but they have to go now, don't you, boys." He made a statement of it rather than a question.

"Oh, I don't know," Ricky began.

"I do," Nick stated firmly. He gave them his *Do what I say because I'm bigger than you look* that usually got their attention.

The boys got the message, but they still laughed as they started shoving each other back and forth while they headed off toward the parking lot.

"I'm betting that those three are a handful," Shannon said.

"You'd win that bet."

"Mind if I ask a question?"

"Mind if I don't answer?" Nick countered. No way was he going to hang around this woman even one second longer than he had to. No one at school had ever seen him with a woman before. Tomorrow was going to be sheer hell. The boys were going to razz him all day long about her.

That was the problem with working at a high school. If a man befriended the students, he left himself open to a lot of good-natured ribbing and pranks when the occasion warranted.

As far as most teenage boys were concerned, any occasion qualified. Any occasion, or none at all.

Nick shuddered to think what the boys would do if they *didn't* like him. At times, working at school was a great deal like *attending* school.

"I'll ask anyway." Shannon said, drawing his attention back to her. "What's with the overalls?" She nodded toward his chest, covered by the denim bib of the overalls in question.

He slipped his hands behind the bib and tapped his fingers against his chest. "What's wrong with overalls?" he demanded.

"Nothing," she said quickly. Boy, the man was touchy. "I just wondered why so many people, including you, are wearing them."

"It's Farmers Day," he told her.

"Oh." Shannon frowned. "Why?"

"What do you mean, why?"

Shannon glanced around at the dozens of people, in addition to Carlucci, who were wearing overalls. "I get the connection between farmers and overalls, but why do you have a Farmers Day? What's the purpose? Local custom? Is the football team called the Tribute Farmers? What?"

He almost smiled. "The Tribute Farmers? You've got a great imagination. You should be a writer."

"Ha-ha. Are you going to answer my question, or should I move along to other things I'd like to ask you?"

He nodded. He would give her what she wanted. This time. "It's a tradition at the high school. It's Homecoming Week. Monday was Cowboy Day, today's Farmers Day. Wednesday is Tie-dye Day, Thursday is Nerd Day."

"Nerd Day?" She laughed.

"Friday is Spirit Day, where everyone wears the school colors."

"How do you dress up like a nerd? Thick glasses and pocket protectors?"

"You got it."

She crossed her arms, intrigued despite herself. "What else goes on during Homecoming Week? Besides the obvious football game."

One side of his upper lip curled in a slight sneer. "What, you writing a book?"

"As a matter of fact, I am."

"About small-town homecomings."

"No, about the various lasting effects of 9/11 on different rescue workers. What you people did, what you went through, takes a toll. I want to write about it, and draw comparisons to the rescue workers at the Oklahoma City bombing."

Nick shook his head, obvious dismay on his face. "Nobody wants to read that stuff. It's done and gone and we've all put it behind us."

Shannon let his attitude roll off as if it were nothing. She had encountered much stiffer resistance than this. Besides, they both knew he was lying through his teeth. At least, she knew it; she hoped he did, too.

"You've put it behind you, have you?" she asked him casually.

"That's right. So I guess you've wasted a trip if that's why you came."

"Are you telling me that day doesn't have anything to do with why you left New York? You don't think about it anymore? You don't have nightmares or flashbacks? You haven't had any alcohol or drug problems since then?"

He opened his mouth, presumably to deny any and all of that, but Shannon held up a hand to stop him.

"Don't bother answering me. We both know you'd lie anyway."

He snapped his mouth shut. She heard his teeth click together. Then he spoke. "I don't lie."

She tilted her head and squinted against the bright afternoon sun. "No?"

"No."

"So, if I were to ask you something like, oh, why did you leave New York, you'd tell me the truth?"

"No."

"No? But you just said you don't lie."

"I wouldn't lie. I wouldn't answer at all."

"Why?"

"Because it's none of your business."

"True. It really isn't."

"Well," he said. "It must be a red-letter day. A reporter admitted the truth."

Shannon reared back. It wasn't the first

time she'd heard a slur against her profession, but she was surprised by the bitterness in his voice. "You should be aware that you and I have something in common."

"I doubt that," he said.

"Oh, but we do. You see," she told him, "I don't lie, either. Not face-to-face, and not in my work. If you'd ever read any of my work, you'd know that."

"Good for you. Now, if you'll excuse me, I'll say goodbye and be on my way."

"Whoa, wait." She reached out and grabbed him by the arm to keep him from leaving. In the next instant, she jerked her hand away and stared at him in shock. She shook her hand as if trying to fling water from her fingertips, hoping that would somehow alleviate the sizzling kick she'd gotten from his arm.

They stood there on the sidewalk beneath the Texas sun staring at each other, breathing hard, braced as if ready to fight or run, she wasn't sure which.

Suddenly Carlucci laughed harshly and stepped back. "This is crazy. I'm going back to work." He turned away, toward the school.

"But school's out for the day."

"Which means I can finally clean up after these little mutants."

"Wait." She leaped after him. "I thought maybe we could talk." She couldn't let him get away so easily.

"We did," he said without slowing down.

"How late will you work?"

"Until I'm finished."

"Carlucci," she said with a growl. "What time do you get off work?"

"At five," he snapped. "Don't be here."

* * *

She was there. He'd seen her drive away at 3:30 p.m. Now it was 4:50 p.m. and she was waiting outside the door for him, with no car in sight. For one impossible instant, he was glad she was there. Then he swore at himself. All she wanted to do was pick his brain, then bare his soul to the world because *the public has a right to know.*

"The hell they do," he muttered. Neither the public nor Lois Lane had a right to look inside him. To pat him on the shoulder and offer their pity while calling him a hero.

He *hated* reporters.

It was a shame, too, because Malloy sure was easy to look at, and he could get used to that sharp sensation that happened when they touched. If it felt that great to touch her, he couldn't imagine what a kiss might do to him. He might be willing to find out, even if she was a reporter.

He wondered how long he could string her along before she gave up on interviewing him and went back to New York. Maybe he shouldn't be refusing her. Maybe he should tell her he'd considered it and see where that took them.

He unclipped the wad of keys from his belt, then stepped outside and locked the door behind himself. "You're back."

She smirked. "Great powers of observation. Maybe you should be a reporter."

"Prompt, and a sense of humor. If you tell me you sew your own clothes I'll have to marry you."

She folded her arms across her chest and

stared at him through narrowed eyes. "I sew my own clothes."

Nick nearly swallowed his tongue. She'd called his bluff. Now what was he going to do?

Her grin turned pure evil. "Cat got your tongue, Carlucci? You're not going to go back on your word, are you? How about we keep it simple and just fly to Las Vegas? My mother will be disappointed, but she'll get over it. What's the matter? You're looking a little green."

"You're a regular comedienne."

"That's what they tell me. So, what do you say? Are you a man of your word, or were you just leading me on?"

He eyed her up and down. "Deal's off. You didn't make those jeans."

"Oh, no, you don't get out of it that easily. You didn't ask if I made *all* my clothes. I've made plenty of them, just not these."

"And you have a great personality."

Her eyes popped wide. "Are you calling me ugly?"

Nick burst out laughing. Considering what he thought of reporters, and the way he had continually dodged this one for months, he couldn't believe how good it felt to joke and laugh with her, and had no idea why he was doing it.

"How many times," she said, "did your mother try to fix you up with some girl who sewed her own clothes and had a great personality?"

He rolled his eyes. "It was my dad and my brother, but it was more times than I care to count."

"Save us all from our well-meaning families," she said with a chuckle.

"You, too?" he asked.

"Oh, yeah. My dad was a cop. A guy had to be pretty sure of himself to knock on my door to pick me up for a date."

"I can imagine. What's he do now, your dad?" Nick asked.

Her smile turned sad. "He died in the line of duty, on 9/11. Same as your dad and brother."

"Ah. Sorry. I didn't know."

She shook her head. "No reason you should have. Is that why you left New York? Because your dad and brother were gone?"

Whatever openness he felt around her slammed shut. "I'll walk you to your car. Where'd you park?"

"Come on, Carlucci," she said quietly. "I'm just curious, that's all. I know what the loss feels like, but it's a simple enough question."

"The answer's not so simple," he said grimly.

"Why?"

"You didn't say where you parked."

She held his gaze for a long time, then sighed. "My car's in the motel parking lot. I walked here."

Relieved that she seemed to have accepted his refusal to answer her question, Nick smirked. "Walked? Your New York is showing."

"What's that mean? It's only a few blocks."

"Nobody walks in Texas. Not on purpose, anyway, or by choice."

She frowned. "Why not?"

"Because that's why God made cars. And horses."

"Hmm. Okay. But you walked to work yesterday."

"And today. I'm a New Yorker, too."

"I'm surprised you walk so much."

"Why? It's not so much," he said.

"It is for somebody the doctors said would never walk again."

Nick wanted to sneer. At the doctors, and at her. Instead he kept his expression bland. "I'd call you a cab, but we don't have any in Tribute, so come on, I'll walk you back to your motel."

She stood where she was and pursed her lips in thought. "No," she finally said. "I'm not going anywhere until you tell me why you left the fire department. I know guys like you. The FDNY was your life. Yet you walked away from it. Why?"

"I left," he said curtly, "because I was no longer fit to serve. I couldn't pass the physical."

She eyed him up and down. "You look pretty fit to me." When he didn't respond, she gave him a hard look. "Does this leave us at a stalemate?" she asked.

"Weren't we always?" He took her by the arm to get her to head down the sidewalk with him, but there was that sharp zap of sensation again when the flesh of his fingers met the bare skin of her arm. This time he held on, and everything seemed to settle.

"Except for that," she said.

"Yeah, well. So, what have you been doing with yourself all day besides badgering me and trying to pick up high-school boys?"

"I haven't begun to badger you," she came back. "When I do, you'll know it. Meanwhile, I spent most of the day touring the town, visiting the shops, and sitting in my room working on my manuscript."

"Tell me about this book you're writing."

He steered her south, toward Main Street. Tribute had only three motels, two at the west end of town, one at the east end, all of them on Main.

"I told you," she said. "It's a 'five years later' look at specific individual 9/11 rescue workers."

"Why?" he asked. "What's the point? It's old news."

"How the work you did affected your life, how you dealt with it in the early days, how you deal with it now."

Nick still didn't get it. "Who wants to read that garbage?"

"You'd be surprised," she said.

"I guess I would," he admitted.

"Okay, look. Here's one angle. At the Oklahoma City bombing back in 1995, during the initial response, everybody pitched in and did everything they could. Later things got organized, and rescue workers worked specific, limited shifts, then were replaced by fresh crews. At the end of every shift, they moved out of the way, to a semiprivate area and unloaded."

"Unloaded what?"

"Whatever they needed to unload, mentally, verbally, whatever. They talked about what they'd seen, the smells, the heat. The frustration of not finding survivors. Anything and everything on their minds. And whatever was said in these meetings stayed there, no exception. At the Twin Towers, the job was so overwhelmingly huge, that type of session wasn't available to the workers. None of you got any counseling until much later. Many of the Oklahoma City guys, despite all the help they had, have ended up with lots of problems—emotional, marital, you name it. If it's been that bad for them, what effects are the New York guys suffering? That's what this book is about."

Nick restrained a sneer, while inside he wanted to weep at the memories she evoked. "So we're supposed to spill our guts so you can write about our poor, pitiful lives, huh?"

She gave a little laugh. "That is pretty much what I made it sound like, isn't it?"

"Pretty much."

"I don't mean it to. It's more of a chronicle. Some of the rescuers I'm including are doing really well, leading totally normal lives."

"And others?"

"Others have had some problems. The same as in the regular population."

"Some people shake it off, some don't?"

"It's not that cut and dried, and you know it," Shannon countered. "Is the man who has trouble merely weak? Or is the one who lets it roll off his back unfeeling and heartless?"

"Your verdict?"

"No verdict. Again, it's not that cut-and-dried. Each individual case is different."

At Main Street, Nick stopped. "Which way to your motel?"

Shannon stared at him and blinked. Was he actually inviting himself to her motel room? They hadn't so much as touched since leaving the school. Yes, being around him excited her, but jumping from how do you do and shaking hands, to doing the motel mamba in one day? "I don't think—"

"Unless you were heading someplace else," he interrupted.

She paused. Maybe she had jumped to conclusions? Maybe her brain was on vacation. "There's no need to walk me," she said. "Unless *you* were heading someplace else?"

He nodded once. "Yeah, there's someplace I need to be pretty soon, but I've still got time to walk you to wherever you're going. Did you think I'd just dump you here on Main and leave you?"

She laughed. "I think I can make it a few blocks down this street in broad daylight without your help."

"I'm sure you can, but I've got better manners than to let you. This way?" He motioned left.

Shannon sighed and shook her head. "Thanks, but I'd just have to turn around and leave as soon as you were gone. I'm hungry. Are you going to eat with me?"

Nick paused. He would very much like to have dinner with her. Any excuse to spend more time with the first woman to interest him in a long, long time. But he didn't want to have to watch every word he said around a reporter, and he'd promised his aunt he'd have dinner with her at home tonight.

"Sorry," he told Shannon. "I can't tonight. How long will you be in town?"

"I'm not sure." Shannon bit back a sigh. Obviously she had misunderstood. He wasn't trying to lure her someplace dark and private for a little one-on-one. Dammit. "I came to do an interview," she told him. "However long that takes."

"Yeah? You might want to think about buying a house in the area, then. If that interview's with me, it could be a while."

"Tell you what," she offered. "I'll let you off the hook for this evening."

"Nice of you."

"If you'll talk to me, really talk to me, tomorrow when you get off work. Over dinner. I'll buy you dinner. How's that?"

Nick almost smiled. "First rule of janitorial work—never turn down a free meal." Besides, he thought, she was probably working on an expense account.

"Good. I'll meet you in front of the school at five. Or did you want to go home and change first?"

"Why would I change? Are you saying you don't want to have dinner with a man who smells like industrial-strength disinfectant? Or maybe it's the tie-dyed shirt I'll have on."

"I don't care what you smell like, or what you wear," she claimed.

"So you say." He laughed. "Give me until five-thirty."

"It's a date."

It was a toss-up as to which one of them looked more startled at the idea.

Chapter Three

With Tribute being such a small town, it shouldn't have surprised Nick that the first words out of his aunt's mouth when he got home were "Well, well, sweetie, you going to tell me who she is?"

To her credit, Beverly wasn't usually a nosy woman, especially for a relative. A female relative, at that. She wasn't demanding information. She was smiling eagerly, hoping, Nick knew, that he'd finally met someone. As in…Someone.

He should have realized that word of a strange woman in town—a woman specifically seeking out Nick—would have arrived home ahead of him. He had not only stood in front of the high school with her, in plain sight of half the town, he'd also introduced her to a trio of big mouths. After that, he had walked her right up to Main Street, for the other half of town to see.

Nothing on earth or in the universe traveled faster than the speed of gossip, and he'd provided plenty of grease.

And dammit, more people than Aunt Bev were going to wonder who she was and what she was doing in town. Beautiful woman like her, people were bound to be curious.

Heck, they'd be curious no matter what she looked like. She was a stranger. That was all it took.

He should have asked her, bribed her, threatened her, whatever it took to get her to keep his past to herself. It was one thing for him to fend off gossip about his love life. His past was another matter entirely.

"She's an acquaintance," he told his aunt. Aunt Bev knew his past better than any person on earth, so she would understand his reticence. "Shannon Malloy. A reporter."

"Reporter?" She looked blank for a moment, then alarmed. "The one who's been leaving you phone messages for months?"

"That's the one."

"Oh, my." She took him by the arm, pulled him into the kitchen and led him to a chair at the table. "Sit down, dear, let me get you a glass of tea."

He was so disconcerted by her obvious concern that he did as she said and watched as she filled a tall glass with ice, then poured sweet tea. The ice cubes cracked and popped.

"What are you going to do?" Aunt Bev asked. She handed him the filled glass.

"Thanks." He took a long swallow. "You mean about the reporter? Not much."

"Not much?" She stood back and put her hands on her hips. "What does that mean, not much?"

Nick sighed. He and Aunt Bev had a standing dinner date every Tuesday night, just the two of them. Sometimes they went out, but usually she cooked. Neither of them had ever canceled on the other. Sharing a house, they of course saw each other all week long, but Tuesday evening was always their special time. He hadn't wanted to drag his current predicament or his past into their time together.

It looked, however, as if Bev was going to insist on it.

"It means," he told her, "that she wants to interview me for a book she's writing, and I have told her no. End of story."

"Ah." Bev nodded and poured herself a glass of tea. "Okay. I guess it makes sense then, since you're not going to let her interview you, that she would hang out at the school, and you would walk her halfway across town."

Nick tipped his glass back and drained it of tea. His aunt had something on her mind, so he would just wait and let her get it out.

She turned away from him and took two

thick pork chops from the refrigerator and set them next to the stove. "After all," she said, still not looking at him. "It would take you several blocks to get your message across, *no* being such a long word, a difficult concept to convey."

He snorted. "Don't look at me. It's all her doing. And you've got that last part right. I've been telling her no for two days, and I'm still not sure she believes me."

Bev turned the heat up beneath the skillet on the stove and poured in enough oil to cover the bottom. "Persistent, isn't she?" she asked. "She doesn't seem to be taking no for an answer."

He smiled. "She'll get the message eventually."

She coated the pork chops in flour, then sprinkled one side with black pepper, the other side with seasoned salt. When the skillet was as hot as she wanted it, she eased the chops in.

She dusted her hands off and turned to face him. "There's another way to get rid of her, of course."

"There is?"

"Talk to her."

"I've been talking to her," he protested. "I've been telling her no, no, no. She just keeps coming back."

Bev shot him a look. "You know that's not what I mean. I mean talk to her, answer her questions. Let her interview you."

"Why in holy hell would I want to do that?"

"You watch your language at my table, young man."

Nick had the good grace—and the brains—to bow his head in remorse. "Sorry."

"Hmph. Apology accepted, even if it wasn't heartfelt. But I wish you'd think about talking to her. Or talk to someone else. Anyone."

"You mean spill my guts and cry and all that cr—…stuff?"

"All right," she said. "If you don't want to talk out your troubles, fine, keep it all bottled up, be miserable. But that doesn't have anything to do with being interviewed. There's no reason you can't answer her questions. Unless you've got something to hide."

"Me?" he protested. "I'm an open book."

"Ha!" She used a long fork to lift one pork chop slightly and peer at the bottom. She must not have been satisfied because she lowered it and turned back to him. "You're as closed up as a clam. You've never talked about what happened when the towers fell."

"Aunt Bev, what else is there to say that hasn't been said already?"

She made a snarling sound that made him purse his lips to keep from grinning.

"You're hopeless," she muttered. "But I still think you should let her interview you. Just because she asks a question doesn't mean you have to answer it."

"I'll keep that in mind when I have dinner with her tomorrow evening."

Bev blinked. Her eyes widened, her mouth opened and made a small O. She looked like a startled kitten. "Dinner?"

Nick tried for nonchalance and thought he might have managed it but for the involuntary twitching of his lips. "She asked me to dinner. I accepted. Now that I have your blessing not to answer her questions, everything should go fine."

"Oh, you stinker." She shook her head sadly and turned back to the stove. "Where did your father go wrong with you? I hope she tricks you into spilling your guts."

Shannon indulged in a chicken-fried steak, mashed potatoes and an artery-clogging serving of creamy gravy.

Sheesh. No wonder gyms, health clubs and diet plans were so popular.

Still, when in Texas… And at a place called Dixie's Diner…

She promised herself this would be her one and only chicken-fried steak on this trip.

She had no trouble at all cleaning her plate, then piously declined to order dessert. *Oh, what a good girl am I.* The walk back to the motel was going to do her good.

It was still daylight when she left the

diner. She didn't feel like cooping herself up in her room for the night. Cooping up meant working, and her head wasn't in it just then. She couldn't stop thinking about Nick Carlucci.

She could easily understand his hesitancy at being interviewed. She'd seen such a thing a hundred times in other people, and it was particularly typical of firefighters and other "hero" types. They were, as a rule, on the shy side. Heroic, adorable, but shy.

But Shannon thought she sensed something other than simple shyness in Nick. In fact, she had yet to detect any shyness at all in the man.

Her research proved that he was no novice at being interviewed. His rescue efforts on 9/11 had nearly cost him his life. Local and national TV reporters had followed the story of his surgery and his miraculous recovery. He'd faced dozens of reporters in those days.

Maybe he'd simply had enough. She couldn't say she blamed him. But that was years ago. She had to make him understand that people wanted to know about him. About how he was, how 9/11 still affected him. If he was doing all right.

Physically, she could tell them, he was doing more than fine. He was looking totally yummy.

Was that why she was still here, even after he'd turned her down for an interview twice? Was she still here because she liked—really liked—the way he looked? Or maybe it was the *zing* she felt when they touched.

She thought about it as honestly as she could until she found herself in the park. Tribute Park, in fact, in the middle of the town square, in front of the courthouse. It was fairly quiet here; but then, the entire town was on the quiet side, as far as she was concerned.

Flower beds lined both sides of the sidewalks that met in the middle of the park. Velvety yellow and purple pansies, and red and white miniature roses were a feast for the eyes. The freshly mowed grass smelled so sweet it made her close her eyes and inhale deeply in order to savor the scent.

More flowers bloomed at the base of a series of smooth, granite monuments. Shannon was drawn to the stones. The first one she came to held the names of all of the local soldiers killed in war, dating back to the Spanish American War.

As was the way of history, the names were all male. Except for the latest edition. A local woman had died while serving with the Texas National Guard in Iraq nearly a year ago.

Nearby stood a second war memorial, this one smaller, and dedicated to local soldiers killed in "the War Between the States." This monument, like the country itself during that particular war, had a line drawn down the center of it. Two local boys who'd died fighting for the Union were listed on the left, while those for the Confederacy on the right numbered nearly a dozen.

Across the center sidewalk stood another monument. Shannon crossed to it, wondering who else the town chose to immortalize in granite. As she read the engravings, she thought, *What a wonderful idea.* This monument honored average citizens who had gone above and beyond in a selfless act to save someone else. A school teacher who'd saved a classroom of students from a tornado in 1901. A grocer who'd lost a leg saving a stranger during a 1923 bank robbery.

Shannon walked along the granite wall, reading of one heroic deed after another. The most recent event was a man who'd donated his organs and, upon his death, had saved the lives of several people and greatly improved the lives of more.

Suddenly she recalled that this was the monument Wade Harrison had erected to honor the organ donor who'd saved his life, as well as other locals who'd made a difference.

Shannon turned and found a wooden bench nearby and took a seat, suddenly wanting to talk to Deedra. At this time of day, her best friend would be at home. Shannon pressed the speed dial button on her cell phone, and a moment later the connection was made.

The two friends wasted no breath on small talk. As was their habit, they jumped right into whatever was on their minds.

"I thought you'd be home by now," Deedra complained.

"I would be—should be—but this guy is being difficult," Shannon admitted.

"What? You can't get a guy to talk to you?"

"Don't overdo the *I'm so shocked* tone," Shannon said.

"Why not? You have to admit, this doesn't happen often. At least not to you. Who is this guy, and why won't he talk?"

Shannon told her about Nick Carlucci. "And it's not that he won't talk to me, he just says he doesn't want to do the interview."

"What else aren't you telling me?" Deedra demanded.

Damn, Shannon thought. "What gave me away?"

"I don't know. Just something in your voice when you say his name."

"Oh, good grief." Shannon groaned. "I'm a cliché now?"

Deedra laughed. "Only to someone who knows you as well as I do."

"Well, then I guess it's a good thing nobody knows me as well as you do."

"I notice you haven't answered me. That means this is going to be good."

"It's not that big a deal."

"Shannon, if it wasn't that big a deal, you would have answered me when I first asked."

"So much for changing the subject," Shannon grumbled.

"That's right. So I ask again. What aren't you telling me about this guy? The way you say his name, I'd almost think you had a big case of the— Oh, you've got to be kidding. You have the hots for this guy? You? Miss I-Never-Fall-for-a-Subject-That-Would-Be-Too-Unprofessional?"

Shannon bit back a laugh at her own expense, to hear her own words thrown back at her. Sort of. "I beg to differ. I never said it would be unprofessional to hook up with an interview subject. I said that I could only do it if I was sure I could keep it separate from the job. As long as I'm freelancing, and as long as both parties agree that sex has nothing to do with the story, and vice versa, then there's no problem."

"Yeah, right. When's the last time that worked out for you?" Deedra asked with laughter in her voice.

"I didn't say it worked, I just said that was my policy. It could work, couldn't it?"

"Sure. Is he good to look at?"

"Oh, yeah. Rugged, chiseled, brooding." Wild horses couldn't make Shannon admit, even to Deedra, that she got a charge—literally—just touching the man. That admission was for later. If ever.

Her skin tingled just thinking about touching him.

"Be still my heart." Deedra let out a dramatic sigh. "I say go for it."

"Of course you do," Shannon said. And she really was thinking about it. She was a big girl, wasn't she? She could handle herself. She could have an affair and keep her heart from getting broken. Hearts wouldn't be involved.

"It's about time you got the hots for somebody," Deedra said. "What I want to know is, what are you going to do about it?"

Shannon groaned, then let out a long sigh. "I'm not sure," she confessed. She knew what she wanted to do. She wanted to jump his bones.

Nick dreamed. This time, no nightmare, but an actual dream. He woke up well before dawn, sweating. He'd dreamed Shannon Malloy had seduced him. He had resisted admirably before giving in and letting her have her way with him.

How was a man supposed to look a woman in the eye after a dream like that? And wasn't it interesting that he couldn't wait to find out?

Let her interview you, Aunt Bev had said.

He considered the ramifications. Agreeing to an interview would allow him to spend time with a woman to whom he was attracted. That, alone, was worth major consideration.

Let her ask her questions. He didn't have to answer every one of them. He didn't have to answer any of them, for that matter. All he had to do was stand his ground, ignore that electricity that arced between them whenever they touched—*simple enough, just don't touch her*—and pay attention to her questions. Reporters were sneaky. They had a way of getting you to say things you hadn't intended to say.

At least, that was Nick's experience. And none of those reporters back in 2001 had had eyes deep enough to drown in.

What the hell. He'd always been a good swimmer.

Wednesday, Shannon had trouble concentrating on her manuscript. She had that First Date with a New Man tingle. She knew it was crazy. Nick Carlucci was an interview subject, not a date. But her nerves didn't seem to care. Neither did that bane of all females, the What Am I Going to Wear organ that lay in the heart of every woman over the age of two.

This occasion, however, was going to be simple. When in Rome…

She found a little shop on Main Street and bought a tie-dyed T-shirt in blues and reds over a white background. She would do her part for Homecoming Week. The clerk congratulated her on her school spirit.

Shannon knew she'd chosen the right clothes when Carlucci walked out of the school at 5:30 p.m., took one look at her shirt and burst out with a huge grin.

He, of course, had obviously cleaned up, as he'd said he would, and changed into a white dress shirt tucked in at the waist of his jeans. He looked…scrumptious.

Down, girl, she told herself. It wasn't that she couldn't afford to mess up her plans for her book, it was that she *refused* to chance harming the project. The book was more than merely important to her, it was vital.

She could do the book, and do a damn good job with it, even if Carlucci refused to be interviewed. She could still include him and write what little she knew, or she could leave him out entirely. The project did not succeed or fail with his inclusion. No one would think the book was not complete.

But, she would. This was her one shot to get this right. And she had to get this right. This book was the only way Shannon knew to honor her father. He'd been there on 9/11, too. Sean Michael Malloy was one of the thirty-seven New Jersey Port Authority police officers who'd answered the call of duty and died that day.

He wouldn't like that, she knew. He would applaud her honoring the rescue workers, both the living and the dead, but not her searching for some part of him in the overall scheme of things. He'd never considered himself a hero, just a man doing his job.

But her father hadn't been able to do that, so it was left to Shannon to speak for him in this matter of looking back, honoring and looking forward.

Oh, yes, she had to get this right. She had to get Nick's cooperation. She squared her shoulders and smiled. He didn't look particularly happy to see her, but she wasn't going to let that stop her. "Hi. Did you manage to work up an appetite?"

He gave her a half smile and slung his weight onto his good leg. "More or less."

He approached her cautiously, but still smiling.

"Where would you like to go for dinner?" she asked him.

"Where, where." With one eye squinted, the other closed, he stared up at the sky and hummed as if deep in thought. "I think... Yes. Carnegie Deli, on Seventh Avenue. Between Fifty-fourth and Fifty-fifth streets."

He wanted to play? She would oblige him. She glanced down at her watch and smiled. "Okay, but they might be closed by the time we get there. It's not the flight, you understand, it's the drive from here to the airport that will slow us down."

They looked at each other and laughed.

Oh, she really liked this man, Shannon

thought. Part of her didn't care if he never agreed to an interview—she would still like him.

But that wouldn't get her book written. She intended to keep her mind on business. Perhaps she could figure out a way to conduct business and pleasure at the same time.

That idea intrigued her.

"What?" Nick asked.

"What, what?" she said.

"You've got a 'cat who swallowed the canary' look in your eyes."

Shannon smiled. "Does that make you nervous?"

He took her hand and placed it on the crook of his arm and, after waiting for the sharp tingling to settle, led her down the sidewalk. "Should it?" he asked with a cocky smile.

She arched a brow. "I was just trying to decide how I want this evening to end."

His smile widened. "What are our options?"

"Our?" Oh, he was smoother than she'd expected. Faster, too.

"Sorry," he said. But he didn't look sorry. He looked smug. Appealingly so, if such a thing was possible. "I just assumed we were spending the evening together."

Shannon listened, but heard not the slightest emphasis on the word *evening.* So why did she feel as if she had lost control?

Interesting. She hadn't set out to control the man, merely the situation. Yet, the man *was* the situation, wasn't he…?

"What?" he asked.

She shook her head and smiled. "Nothing. Yes. We're spending the evening together.

Now, you know the town better than I do. Where should we go for dinner?"

"That depends on what you want to eat. Would you prefer steak, barbecue, Mexican food or Italian? Or good ol' down-home cooking?"

"It all sounds good. Any recommendations?"

They stopped next to her car at the end of the sidewalk.

"Well," he said, "you can't go back to New York without eating some honest to goodness Texas barbecue."

"Then Texas barbecue it is." On a whim, she tossed her keys in the air. "You take the wheel, Nick."

Chapter Four

The woman was one surprise after another, and Nick was more intrigued by her and interested in her than he would have thought possible.

Don't forget "turned on by" while we're at it, pal.

Not likely, he thought. No way he could forget the hot, sharp attraction, even through all the laughter and surprises.

The first surprise had been the tie-dyed T-shirt. She'd gone to some trouble, he'd bet, to come up with that. He doubted she carried one in her suitcase.

The pearls were a surprise, too. Pearls and a T-shirt? But she made it work.

Surprise number three was that she'd tossed him her car keys. He hadn't expected that. She was a woman who seemed to know what she wanted and how she planned to get there. Letting someone else take charge, even for something so simple as driving them to dinner, didn't fit with the woman he'd been coming to know.

The next surprise was how well she took the news that the restaurant he was taking her to was a few miles out of town. He had expected at least a token argument. After all, she didn't know him well.

She'd merely smiled and said, "Okay."

"Okay?" he'd asked. "What if I turn out to be the neighborhood ax murderer planning to dump your body out of town after I chop you up?"

She'd sputtered with laughter. "Are you?"

"That's a question you should have asked before we got in the car."

"That's okay," she'd told him with a big smile. "I'll take my chances."

He wanted to get suspicious—she was being way too nice and agreeable for a reporter—but then she surprised him again when he pulled up in front of Bigg Bobb's Bar-B-Que.

At a first brief glance, it appeared to be a seedy, run-down converted gas station. But if you really looked, and judging by Shannon's wide eyes and wider smile, she must have, you saw that while yes, it was a converted gas station, Bigg Bobb's was well maintained. Bobb had taken the gas-station theme to heart and turned the two garage bays into a dining room. Inside, the walls were decorated with 1950s-era oil company signs, other memorabilia from the same decade, dozens of green plants, and the best advertisement of all, the ever-present aroma of hickory smoke and barbecue sauce.

The sign over the door read: If You Don't Like Cajun Music, You Might As Well Go Home. If You Don't Like BBQ, We Don't Want To Know You.

Once he and Shannon had placed their orders, over the promised wail of Cajun music, Shannon continued to surprise him by not turning into Barbara Walters right away. She didn't ask him any questions that weren't general in nature, about Bigg

Bobb's, the town, the school. She seemed particularly interested in Homecoming.

"Tomorrow you wear the school colors?" she asked.

"For the parade if you want, yeah. But at school it's Nerd Day."

"That's pocket protectors, right?"

"We're growing on you," he said.

"How's that?"

"You said pocket protectors with a perfectly straight face, as if kids wear them to school every day."

"I'm laughing on the inside." Her lips twitched. "So then, school colors for the parade, and again the next day at school. So why do you have the parade on Thursday? Why not wait until Friday, when everyone will be in the right colors?"

"We used to, but the football coach said

it interfered with his pregame psychology, or something like that. Too much going on, takes the players' focus off the game. And no, you can't the team away from the parade because they're the star attraction."

"Hmm. Okay. So what are the school colors? What's your mascot? No, wait. The Tribute Tigers?"

She'd surprised him again. "Good guess. How'd you know?"

"It's a writer thing. Alliteration. It needed to start with a *T,* and somehow, the Tribute Turtles just doesn't cut it."

"We could have been the Tribute Tornadoes," he offered.

She tilted her head and smiled at him. "You like it here, don't you." She was stating, not asking.

"Define *here*."

"It doesn't matter. This restaurant, the town, the state. You like all of it."

"You sound surprised."

"I guess I am. Snobbish of me, I know. I guess I just thought you would be homesick for New York by now. Don't you miss it?"

Something inside him broke loose—no, broke free—and allowed him to open up a little to her. "Yes, I like it here, but, yes, I miss New York."

"Okay," she said slowly. "Now you've got me curious."

Their waiter saved him. "Who ordered the rack?"

"The what?" Shannon asked.

"Rack of ribs," Nick explained. "And they're mine. The lady ordered the brisket."

"Oh," Shannon said like a woman drooling

over her long-lost lover. "This looks and smells…divine."

Nick had a sharp urge to have her look at him that way. "Wait till you taste it," he said, making himself want to look at and smell and taste her, up close and personally. Inch by inch.

Damn, he needed to get his mind off sex before he did or said something inappropriate. This was just a friendly dinner between two people who barely knew each other.

Not that such a thing would stop him, if she gave him any encouragement.

"I assume you're no stranger to ribs?" he asked.

She laughed. "What you're really asking is, do I realize you're going to eat with your fingers, and clean up with your tongue."

Nick choked. "Uh…"

"Oops." Her smile turned sheepish, her face red. "I didn't mean that the way it sounded."

Nick was damn sorry about that. He cleared his throat. "I'm, uh, going to lick my fingers."

She closed her eyes and inhaled deeply. "You're not helping, Carlucci."

He stared at her until she opened her eyes and met his gaze.

Whatever he might have said just then—and he wasn't sure what words would have come out of his mouth, considering the hot scene playing out in his head—but their waitress returned to refilled their drinks, cutting him off.

He and Shannon looked at each other and smiled.

"Saved by the iced tea," she told him.

"For now," he said.

Her lips quirked. "Promise?"

* * *

Shannon couldn't remember the last time she had enjoyed herself so much. The place, the service, the food, each of them would have been wonderful on its own, but roll them all together and throw in Nick Carlucci, and nothing, as far as she was concerned, could top it.

Who knew the man could tease and joke so much? Who knew that he could be so charming or that she could still be charmed?

Plus, he was more open than she'd thought he would be. That might be because they weren't talking about anything truly personal. Other than a few sexual innuendos. So far.

That was about to change.

She waited until his second order of ribs came out—it was all-you-can-eat rib night at Bigg Bobb's, and he seemed to be taking full advantage of the offer—then she forked another tender bite of her brisket. "How did you ever find Tribute, Texas, anyway? Do you have family here?"

He studied her through narrowed eyes, then shook his head. "I told myself that when you started asking real questions, if I answered at all, I would give you a simple yes or no, at best."

"Did I ask a real question?"

"You know you did."

"All right. I know I did. What I'm wondering is, how did you know I did? It's a pretty casual question, did you move here to be near family. Something anyone would ask, if they were curious."

"Something your readers will want to know?"

"For right now," she told him honestly, "it's

what I want to know. What makes you think it's for any other purpose?"

"Your eyes changed."

She blinked. "My eyes changed?"

"Your ears grew, all the better to hear me with."

Shannon huffed out a breath. "You're making fun of me. Never mind. Let's back up a minute. You said you'd planned to give me a yes or no."

"That's right."

"So, why didn't you?"

He pulled another rib from the rack on his plate. "Why didn't I what?"

"Oh, man, it's a good thing I like this brisket too much to throw it at you. You'd try the patience of a saint. Why didn't you give me a yes or no when I asked if you had family here?"

Nick licked a dab of barbecue sauce off the spot between his thumb and forefinger. Slowly. He watched her while he did it. She watched him do it.

Satisfied that they were both still churned up, he answered her. "Because it would have been misleading."

She swallowed, gratifying him with her need to collect herself before she could speak.

"Misleading how?"

"You asked *do* I have family here, and the answer to that is yes. But considering the question right before that, about how I found Tribute, I had to assume you wanted to know if I came here because I had family here. The answer to that would be no."

"Okay, you're going to torment me with semantics. Fine."

"You're a writer. You play with words all the time."

"I try to use the ones that say what I mean. And you're right. I was ambiguous. I'll start over. Why did you move to Tribute?"

Nick hesitated and thought before he spoke. She wasn't technically interviewing him, not taking notes or using a recorder, but he couldn't kid himself. There was no such thing as "off the record" for a reporter. Anything and everything he told her about himself and his life would become fodder for her book. As long as he said only what he wouldn't mind other people reading about, he'd be fine. He could handle her questions.

"When my aunt's husband died, she wanted to come back to the place she had lived when they were first married, and she wasn't ready to live alone."

"So you came with her?"

"That's right."

"And took a job at the school."

"That's right."

She cocked her head and studied him again as if trying to make up her mind whether or not to believe him. "Does your aunt still live here? Wait." Her eyes widened and she smiled. "She's the reason you wouldn't have dinner with me last night. You had dinner with her."

Was he that easy to read? Nick jammed a forkful of potato salad into his mouth and wished she would do the same.

"That's right," he finally said after swallowing his food.

"I'm so glad you decided to give me more than a simple yes or no," Shannon told him. There was sarcasm in her voice. He wasn't sure why until she added, "*That's right* is so much more communicative. You want to be careful not to talk my ear off with it, though."

"You're funny," he told her. "I like that about you."

She smiled at him. "You do? Well, I like that about you. That you like me. What do you know? We like each other."

Nick might have been out of the game for a while—okay, for years—but there was nothing wrong with his radar. She had just tossed him an opening. He wasn't about to let it pass.

"I know a way," he said, watching her carefully, "that we could get to like each other a whole lot better." End of salvo. The ball was in her court now.

Return serve. "You're sure we'd both like it, and like each other even better?"

"Oh, yeah," he said with feeling. "A *whole* lot better."

She thought about it a moment, then sat back in her chair to let the waitress clear away her plate. Then there were drinks to refill. Then there was dessert to order. Napkins to fiddle with. Water to sip.

Just when he was doubting she would ever respond, she finally looked him in the eye. "What do you have in mind?"

Nick chuckled and gave her an exaggerated leer. "Well, since you asked…"

She rolled her eyes and groaned. "Don't be such a guy."

"But I am a guy," he protested.

"What I mean—"

"Do you have any idea how much it turns me on when you act all prissy like that?"

"Prissy?" Her voice dropped to a low growl. "You think I'm *prissy?*"

He couldn't have kept the grin off his face if he'd tried. "I said you *acted* prissy, which you do on occasion. But your eyes say it's a lie. What I mean," he mimicked. "That was good."

Nick had never met a woman he wanted more than he wanted Shannon just then. Somewhere, sometime, he must have done something right, to have her pop into his life. "I got lucky," he muttered.

"Excuse me?" Shannon said, her brow arching.

The waitress stopped with her bottomless pitcher of iced tea and refilled their glasses. "Did I hear that right?" she asked with a wink in his direction. "You getting lucky tonight, sugar?"

Nick slid down in his chair and covered his face with one hand. If he'd kept his mouth shut…he had to quit talking to himself.

"So he says," Shannon told her.

"That's not what I—" he began.

"Think he'll get what he wants?" the waitress asked with the biggest smirk Nick had ever seen, from what he could see between his fingers that still covered his face. At least he didn't think he knew the woman.

"I don't know," Shannon said as if in deep consideration. "At the very least, I'm going to make him wait for it. Maybe beg."

"Atta girl."

"Why, thank you," Shannon told her.

Nick still covered his face, waiting for the waitress to leave.

"She's gone. You can come out now."

Nick lowered his hand and smirked. "Are we having fun?"

She snickered. "I am."

He looked at her, her sweet mouth, her deep blue eyes, her light brown hair. Every feature was, to him, perfect. Had he noticed before that a row of freckles dotted her nose and cheeks?

"Nick? Is something wrong?"

"Wrong? No," he told her. "Right now everything is just right."

A slight shiver moved over her.

Nick smiled.

They headed back to town in silence, nothing but the sound of tires humming sixty miles an hour down the blacktop. Every few minutes, there was lightning, followed a few seconds later by a boom of thunder. A storm was moving in.

Shannon's mind and pulse raced nearly as fast as the tires. She felt as if she were standing on the edge of a cliff. It wasn't the storm that had her on that edge—it was anticipation. Behind her, figuratively speaking, lay sameness and familiarity. Safety. Before her, the unknown. And Nick. And maybe, just maybe, excitement like she'd never known.

Each time the lightning flashed, it illuminated the interior of the car with an oddly harsh light, throwing Nick's face in sharp relief, his eyes in deep shadow, the hollows of his cheeks, black slashes. For just a second, in that light, he looked like every fantasy she'd ever had.

Did he really want her, or had she misread him?

No, he'd wanted her. She'd been sure of that a few minutes ago, so there was no reason to doubt him now. He still wanted her if the rigid set to his jaw and his white-knuckled grip on the steering wheel were any indications.

"You're awfully quiet." She spoke softly, but her voice sounded loud in the car.

"So are you," he said.

"I loved Bigg Bobb's," she said, watching him from the corner of her eye. "But I'm going to need a shower to get rid of all the barbecue sauce."

His mouth curved. "A shower, huh? If I ask if you need any help with that, will you slap my face?"

"Boy, give the man a little barbecue and he gets all risqué on me."

"Hey, you started it," he said, protesting.

"Are you complaining?"

"Are you kidding?" he asked incredulously. "No, ma'am. I'm thanking my lucky stars."

Shannon laughed. "That might be the sweetest thing anybody's ever said to me. Except, I don't see any stars."

Another dance of lightning lit the night.

"Maybe I have lucky lightning," he said with a smile. "But if it's sweet you want—" He slowed for the speed zone just this side of town. "I can do sweet."

"Really?" The thunder from the last lighting finally rumbled. The storm was still several miles away. "Give me a sample of sweet."

"Sugar," he said in a dark, silky voice.

He wasn't even looking at her. With nothing but his voice, he was melting her bones. If she didn't get him up to her room—

"Maple syrup."

Shannon blinked. "Huh?"

"Honey. You wanted sweet, I'm giving you sweet. Chocolate cake. Chocolate milk."

Do I feel like an idiot, or what? He was teasing her. And she'd fallen for it, big time. Shannon laughed until tears formed. Laughed at herself, and at him. "Oh, heavens, and I thought you were the quiet, sullen type."

"I've been known to be quite sullen," Nick responded, tongue in cheek. "But you just bring out the best in me." And that, he thought, was the startling truth. He felt different around her. He hesitated even to think it, but what he felt was…better. Not just felt better, but felt like a better person. More alive.

No, alive wasn't it. Vital, that was it. He felt more vital. As if he mattered. He felt more his old self around her. He wasn't sure what it meant, but he wasn't ready to see an end to it yet.

He flipped on the blinker and turned into the parking lot of the Tribute Inn. Another flash of lightning crossed the sky, then another and another in quick succession.

The original Tribute Inn, Nick had been told, had been carried off by a tornado about ten years ago and, along with several other nearby buildings, dumped in about a zillion pieces all across the county. All the buildings had been rebuilt from the ground up. The motel was a simple structure, two stories, built in an L. All rooms faced the parking lot. The office took up the downstairs outside corner farthest from the street.

"Where do you want me to park?" he asked her.

"My room's in the middle corner back

there, upstairs. There's a staircase there." She pointed to the middle of the building.

He frowned. "One staircase?" The fireman in him didn't like the looks of that.

"There's another at the other end, but it's farther to my room from there."

Ah. Okay. The only thing that would make it better, in his view, was if each room had a back door. That, of course, was too much to ask.

The parking lot was about half-full, but there was an empty space just down from her staircase. He pulled in, shut off the lights and engine, then sat back.

The sudden quiet was startling.

What now? she thought frantically. All night it seemed as if she had forever to make a decision about getting involved with Nick, but she had just run out of time. With her heart thumping in her throat, she wondered what she was supposed to do. All she really knew was that she did not want to spend this night as she normally did—alone. She was so very tired of alone. Funny how she hadn't realized that until just then, sitting in a rented car with a man who made her pulse race. She barely knew him, but that didn't seem to matter.

Good grief, she was twenty-nine years old. Surely she should be able to invite a man to her room without falling apart.

In the movies "Come up for a drink" always worked, but she didn't have anything to drink but tap water.

"Are you ready to go up?" he asked.

At the sound of his voice, she jerked as if shot. "Up?"

"To your room. Or maybe you'd rather sit here for a while? But a storm's coming. You probably don't want to get trapped in your car and have to wait it out."

The storm, she thought. She couldn't possibly send him to walk home and perhaps get caught out in the rain. She *had* to invite him up, didn't she? Of course she did.

The decision made, she felt much steadier. As long as she didn't think too much about what was likely to happen while they waited out the storm.

"Would you like to come up for a while?" she asked him.

He studied her so long that her nerves stretched tighter. She was about to give up hope that he would answer, when finally he said, "Yes. I'd like that very much.'

The deep softness sent a shiver down her spine.

He got out and came around the car to open

her door. He extended his hand to help her out and when she took it that sharp quiver of sensation hit them both. But this time, instead of letting go and jumping away from each other, they held on, their eyes locked.

After a long moment, he tugged gently, and she stepped out. They climbed the stairs side by side and, for the first time, she saw him truly favor his leg. Stairs were definitely hard on him. She wanted to ask if he was all right, but held her tongue. He wouldn't appreciate the concern, she knew.

At the top of the stairs his gait smoothed out after a couple of steps, until his limp was once again barely noticeable.

Lightning flashed again. The thunder came more quickly this time. The storm was getting closer.

She made herself look forward during that

brief flash of brilliant light. She feared that if she looked at Nick and saw that sharp light on that strong, tense face, she might have a meltdown right there on the walkway.

By the time they reached her door, her heart was about to pound its way out of her chest. Not from exertion, but from anticipation, and maybe a wild case of nerves.

The Tribute Inn used actual metal keys for its guest rooms. Simple enough, in theory, but she couldn't seem to fit hers into the lock. That might have had something to do with the way her hands were trembling, as if she had the palsy.

"Need help?"

She laughed. "I'd say no, I've been putting keys in locks all my life, but tonight I don't seem—"

He put his hands on her shoulders and

turned her to face him. "It's all right, Shannon. We don't have to do this if you don't want to. It's okay to change your mind."

Flash. Lightning traced highlights and shadows on his face, this time giving him a predatory look that called to her so sharply she nearly gasped. Instead, she swallowed. "Do you *want* me to change my mind? Have you changed your mind?"

"Not on your life, lady," he said with feeling.

"Then would you please open this door?" She handed him her key and stepped aside to let him at the lock.

Nick wasted no time in getting them inside her room. He wasn't going to ask again if she was sure. He'd asked and she had answered yes more than once. She could still say no, but she would have to think of it on her own.

He closed the door and leaned back against

it, taking her into his arms and pulling her close against his chest. She felt good there. Small and slight, yet solid, too. And warm. Holding her close made his heart pound. But it was her mouth he wanted at that moment.

The room was pitch-black. He wanted to see her, to look in her eyes while he tasted her mouth. With one hand, he fumbled beside the door until he found the switch.

The lamp beside the bed cast a halfhearted pool of light ten feet from where they stood at the door, but it was enough that Nick could see her.

"That's better," he whispered. Then he lowered his head and took her mouth with his. The kiss was hot and deep and sent his pulse pounding and his blood racing. He'd wanted to keep his eyes open so as not to miss any part of the experience of kissing her. But her eyes were closed, and he felt his closing, too, the more to concentrate on the softness of her lips, the rough-smooth texture of her teasing tongue.

Oh, yes, this was what he wanted. *She* was what and who he wanted. The surprise, the sheer relief to know that he could still feel these sensations, when he hadn't felt much of anything for the past five years, exhilarated him. He drank her in and took everything she gave, and she was generous.

But she took, too, and demanded more. He answered her with his lips and tongue and teeth, and set his hands loose to roam over her, to feel her shape, her softness, her firmness, her curves. Her breasts. It had been years since he'd had the privilege of touching a woman's breasts. Hers were a perfect fit in his palms. He wondered if she would mind if he never took his hands away. He flexed his fingers on them and nearly groaned at their firm resilience.

Shannon felt her blood rush to her breasts. They seemed to swell to fill his hands. Heaven help her, she wanted those hands on her flesh, and her hands on his skin. She tugged at his shirt, pulling the tail free of his jeans. In the process, she dropped her purse and kicked off her shoes. And somehow, her new tie-dyed T-shirt ended up on the floor. She believed it had help, but not from her, and she was thankful.

In a flash she had his shirt unbuttoned and Nick had removed her bra. Then, from waist to shoulders, her bare flesh was pressed against his, and everything inside her turned warm and liquid, like honey in the sun. Never had she felt anything so strong, so peaceful yet stirring, arousing. Finally, finally she was not alone. She felt as if she never would be again.

She never wanted to move. Until his hand slipped into her jeans. "Oh, *yes,*" she whispered against his lips.

Nick's pulse leaped at her response to his touch. At the rate his body was going, he would be lucky to get them to the bed without losing control.

"Come," she whispered with a little pull on his arms.

"I will," he said with feeling. "Probably sooner than you'll appreciate."

She sucked in a sharp breath and stopped halfway to the bed and kissed him. "I doubt it." She ran her hands over his bare chest and took his breath away.

Such a simple thing, a hand on a chest. But

it was a woman's hand—*this* woman's hand—on *his* chest, and it was far from simple. It was erotic. It was hot. It was thrilling. It was comforting. It was soothing. How could anything be erotic and soothing at the same time?

And yet, her touch was. He understood the erotic and was grateful for it. Maybe the soothing was for finally feeling this way again after all these years. To know he was still capable of pleasing a woman, of being pleasured by one. That this essential part of his manhood was not lost to him after all.

When she flicked her fingernails over his nipples, he forgot to wonder about anything. With a moan, he kissed her hard and deep and shuffled the two of them to her bed.

Four hands tugged and pulled and fumbled, breaths rasped, clothes ended up on the floor. And finally Nick and Shannon lay on the bed together, naked, wrapped in each other's arms.

"Oh, yeah," he said, running a hand over her satiny hip. "I like your skin."

Shannon took in a long, deep breath and tried to slow her racing pulse. She spread her hands across his back. "Yours is pretty prime, too." She kissed his shoulder, then nipped her way along his collarbone, loving the salty taste of his skin.

Nick nearly lost his mind. What she was doing felt so good, he wanted to shout. He doubted he had enough air in his lungs for it, but he could think of better uses for his mouth anyway. Her lips were smooth against his skin, her tongue hot. Her teeth took tiny bites that sent electrical impulses from his collarbone to his groin. He shifted until he could put his mouth on her shoulder and returned the favor.

Shannon shivered. She had never felt so greedy. She wanted to take in all of him at once. She wanted to run her hands smoothly over him, but ended up grasping him instead, afraid to go slowly, afraid to be gentle, for fear he might somehow disappear. She grasped, and held on. His biceps felt like warm, carved marble. She'd never felt anything better.

Unless it was his shoulders, or his chest. She touched him everywhere she could reach. Kissed him every place her lips could find.

They drove each other on until their skin slicked with sweat. To Nick, she felt like a sensuous fire come to life in his arms, a fire that scorched him clear through and had him begging for more. He couldn't seem to get enough of her and knew he wouldn't until he buried himself deep inside her.

He felt and found her ready. Some deep part of his brain kicked in and reminded him to reach for the condom he carried in his wallet. When it was on, he settled himself between her thighs, then held still, his upper body braced on his forearms.

Shannon looked up at him in the pale gold light from the lamp and felt singed by the heat in his eyes. Why was he waiting? She wrapped her legs around his hips and arched toward him. Didn't he know how much she wanted him? Couldn't he tell that she was going to die, right there in the bed, if she couldn't feel him inside her?

"Nick," she whispered.

"Yes," he whispered back. He wanted to savor this moment, to make it last. He knew that once he entered her, he was going to lose all control and race toward the finish. He had to make sure she was with him. But the look in her eyes and the feel of her smooth, strong legs wrapped around him wouldn't let him wait. Neither would the urgency in her voice. It matched what he felt inside. She was with him.

With one small flex of his hips, he nudged against her slick heat.

"More," she demanded.

Nick smiled. "You said the magic word." Another flex, this one deeper. Then deeper still until he was in all the way.

Beneath him, she moved, raising her hips, moving them side to side. Moaning.

"Are you with me?" he managed to say on a strangled breath.

"I will be." She raised her arms and pulled him down for a long, hot kiss. "If you'll hurry. Otherwise I'll be ahead of you."

He laughed. "No way." He didn't think he'd ever laughed at such a time before, but just then, with her, it felt right. He reached both hands beneath her head and threaded his fingers into her hair, anchoring himself, tilting her head up for another kiss, and began to move. In and out, as slowly as he could.

But the heat was already overwhelming, and the new friction was the spark that shot them both over the edge in mere moments.

Still holding each other, they rolled to lie on their sides, facing each other, so he wouldn't crush her with his weight. There they gasped for breath and grinned at each other.

Chapter Five

The thunderstorm blew through town around midnight, and the next day the air was fresh and clear and just cool enough to require a sweater, with the tang of turning leaves in the air. The perfect autumn day for a homecoming parade.

Shannon strolled along Main from her motel toward the town square. Nick had said that would be the best place from which to watch the parade.

At the mere thought of his name, a hot flush raced from her head to her toes and back again. She may have miscalculated. She'd been so sure that she could ease into a casual affair with him, a little mutual scratching of itches, no big deal, just a good time being had by all.

Except her night with Nick had been a very big deal. Quite possibly the biggest deal of her life. How was she supposed to look him in the eye today, when she felt her entire world had slipped off-kilter? Would he be able to look at her and know he had reached something deep inside of her that no man had ever reached before? She was afraid the emotions inside her—confusion, elation, fear, anticipation—showed on her face. And maybe frustration, too, because she knew he hadn't felt the same things she had.

Oh, he had no complaints about the sex. They had been dynamite together. Three times.

But she felt as if he'd been holding some part of himself back. While she had opened herself completely. She hadn't meant to; it had just happened. His hands had fisted in her hair, his dark eyes, heavy-lidded, eating her alive, their bodies joined, and she had been overwhelmed by sensations and emotions. Her climax, when it had hit, had been more powerful than anything she'd ever felt. Until the next one, and the one after that. Nick Carlucci should wear a sign warning women to beware. One night with him, and they'll never be the same.

What Shannon had to decide was what to do about these new feelings she had for him.

"Are you cold?"

She nearly jumped out of her skin. "You scared ten years off my life."

Nick looked at her curiously. "You're standing on Main Street with dozens of people all around. That must have been some mental trip you were on. Is everything okay?"

The hand she held against her chest told her her heart was still in there, but it had a long way to go in slowing down to normal. "Sure," she lied. "Fine."

Or maybe not, she thought. She glanced around and realized she had walked all the way to the park without realizing where she was. Without noticing the dozens of pedestrians lining the sidewalks. A number of high schoolers and a few adults, too, sported black-rimmed glasses and plastic pocket protectors filled with ink pens, all in honor of

Nerd Day. Most people were decked out in red and white—even Nick wore a red-and-white team jacket with leather sleeves.

She shook her head. She must have really been out of it. She wondered if she would have noticed if there'd been a fire.

"I guess my mind wandered," she admitted.

Nick's dark, bedroom eyes slid to half-mast and took on a seductive look. "To anyplace in particular?"

Shannon sucked in a deep breath. A certain look, a tone of voice. Was that all it took to have her ready to beg for more of what they'd shared last night? *Get a grip, girl.* She straightened her shoulders and steadied herself.

"No," she answered him. "Just taking in the sights. Where did all these people come from? What did they do, shut down every business in town?"

He gave her an easy smile. "Close to it, I guess. Everybody has somebody, family or friend, connected to the high school. Homecoming parade's a big deal around here."

"So I see." She pulled a small digital camera from her shoulder bag. "I'm ready."

He frowned as if in deep thought. "You going to write a book about it?"

She hadn't thought to but the idea wasn't half-bad. "An article, maybe. Does that bother you?"

"No. Not at all." He gave her a halfhearted smile. "I'd rather see you write that than the other thing you're working on."

"Why doesn't that surprise me? But I doubt I can make an entire book out of a homecoming parade, and my publisher is expecting that 'other thing,' as you put it."

He grimaced. "As far as I'm concerned, a

book about Homecoming would be a better use of paper."

Shannon started to laugh it off, but something tweaked in the back of her mind. Maybe not an article about the parade. Maybe a book about the entire Homecoming Week, small-town style? She could visit other small towns, get a cross section from different parts of the country....

"There's that look again," Nick said. "You're gone."

She blinked, shook her head and smiled. "No, I'm here. But you've given me a possibly great idea for a book."

"About Homecoming?"

"Maybe."

He looked skeptical. "You're joking, aren't you?"

"I don't know. It's just an idea. What's

with the letter jacket? I thought you were the custodian."

"I help out with football practice, sometimes at games."

"Really? Doing what? Coaching?"

"Not really. Mostly I help out with first aid. I've got a lot of experience there."

"Oh. I guess you do. Is that the band I hear? Is it time?" She made her way to a spot at the curb and Nick followed.

It had been a long time since Shannon had seen a homecoming parade. She wasn't quite sure what to expect.

She could hear the marching band clearly now, but they weren't leading the parade. First came a local police car with its lights flashing. Every few feet, the cop hit the siren for a couple of seconds, then cut it off. The crowd cheered.

And it was a crowd, Shannon noted. People two and three deep lined both sides of the street for the three blocks of the official parade route, with a small knot of onlookers gathered in the grass behind Shannon's curb spot, another group just down the street at the gas station. People stood; some sat on lawn chairs they'd brought from home; some sat on the curb; and others sat on top of cars and on tail-gates of pickups. She shot pictures of the crowd and the cop.

After the squad car came a truck pulling two long, flatbed trailers sporting the Tribute Tigers football team, some perched, some lounging, on hay bales. Some looked en-dearingly embarrassed, while others mugged and clowned around for all they were worth, putting on a great show for everyone with a camera—and there were lots of cameras. Every proud parent in the crowd wanted to capture the moment the Tigers rode through town in the parade.

"That's your team, huh?" Shannon asked.

"That's them," Nick confirmed.

"Are they going to win tomorrow night?"

"They're supposed to."

"Well of course they're supposed to. Are they going to, that's the question."

"If you ask them, they say yes," Nick said.

Behind the players came the cheerleaders, leaping and kicking and cheering. They stopped right in front of the park, and Shannon and Nick, and performed one of their cheers, stirring up the crowd with school spirit.

Shannon took pictures while she cringed.

"Why the face?" Nick asked.

"I read an article. Cheerleading injuries

have more than doubled in the last decade. I wish they wouldn't do those flips. And on pavement." But she snapped more shots.

"I take it you weren't a cheerleader."

"Me? Ha. I was a geek. School newspaper, yearbook committee, that kind of stuff."

"A geek, huh?" He grinned. "I'll have to think about that."

"I wish you wouldn't," she muttered.

"I can see you with a set of pom-poms."

"Watch out, Carlucci, you're bigger than I am, but I can still hurt you."

"Woman's got no sense of humor," he grumbled.

The cheerleaders finished their yell and flipped and tumbled their way down the street. The pep squad followed, marching in semi-straight rows, belting out another cheer.

Then came the majorettes, leading the way

for the drum major and the marching band, who played a jazzy rendition of "The Eyes of Texas Are Upon You," with the horns and reeds bopping side to side in time with the music.

Shannon shot pictures of it all, stooping, stretching, jumping out into the street, whatever necessary to get the best shot. Her face was alive with fun and excitement. Nick was getting a bigger kick out of her enjoyment than he was from the parade itself.

He'd been apprehensive about facing her today, after the night they'd spent. He didn't know what to expect from her, or what she would expect from him. *Nice ride, see you later?* Or, *how about another round?* Or something in between; but for the life of him, he couldn't imagine what might be in between.

But she didn't seem ill at ease, so that was something.

On the other hand, she had yet to acknowledge that anything had happened between them, much less the most spectacular sex he'd ever experienced. If she thought it wasn't worth a comment, that was troubling.

After the band finished "The Eyes of Texas," it started up with the school fight song.

Three bars into it, Shannon laughed. "That's my school song."

"Get out," Nick said.

"No, really. Yours is probably 'Red and White Forever.' Ours was 'Green and White Forever, Loyal are we,'" she sang. "Wow. I haven't heard that song in years."

When the song was over, the crowd cheered and the band marched on. The crowd cheered again and laughed at the antics of the school mascot.

The Tribute Tiger, in all his—or her—

glory—red and white, rather than black and orange—was hamming it up big time for the crowd, throwing candy, dancing around, running from one side of the street to the other, and thoroughly entertaining the onlookers.

"Oh, look," Shannon said with a squeal. "Your tiger has a pocket protector stuck to its chest. You have a nerdy tiger."

"What can I say?" Nick answered. "It's Nerd Day."

The parade wound up with a half-dozen teenagers on horseback, sporting a 4-H and FFA banner on a pole.

Shannon shot a few more pictures, then stowed her camera. "That was fun." Shannon tilted her face up to the sun and smiled. So far, the day was a definite ten.

"There's my boy."

A woman in her late fifties or early sixties,

decked out in the red-and-white Tribute Tigers school colors, strolled up to Nick and planted a big red kiss on his cheek. Grinning, she used her thumb in a practiced gesture to wipe the lipstick off of him.

"Are you going to introduce me to this lovely lady?" the woman asked sweetly.

Nick smiled sadly and shook his head, the perfect picture of long-suffering patience. "Could you be any less subtle?" He put his arm around the woman's shoulder and smiled. "Shannon, this is my aunt, Beverly Watson. Aunt Bev, Shannon Malloy, ace reporter from New York."

Shannon returned the woman's smile and the two of them shook hands.

"I've been hearing—"

"—about you." They spoke at the same time, then laughed.

"Don't listen to him," Shannon said. "I'm really a nice person."

"Now, dear, he hasn't said—"

"Wait." Shannon held a hand up to stop her. "I don't mean to put you in the middle. But I know what he thinks of reporters, so don't try to cover for him."

"I wouldn't dream of it." Beverly got a definite twinkle in her eye. "Has he agreed to be interviewed yet?"

"No," Shannon said with a dark look for Nick.

"Well, then, why don't the two of you come around for dinner this evening, and you and I can double-team him."

Surprise held Shannon quiet for a moment. His aunt was on her side? "You mean you think he should let me interview him?"

"Yes, and I've told him so, but he's stubborn."

"Stubborn? Not Nick."

"The stories I could tell you." Beverly raised her gaze to the sky as if beseeching the heavens for aid.

"Ladies, please." Nick wore a decidedly pained look on his face. "No female bonding allowed on Main Street."

"You'll live." Shannon patted his shoulder.

Beverly patted his other shoulder at the same time and said, "There, there, you poor, put-upon thing, you. Will lasagna make you feel better?"

He gave a beautiful imitation of a sad five-year-old, his head drooping, one side of his mouth twisted. "Maybe."

"With cheesecake for dessert?" his aunt tempted.

He peered at her with one hope-filled eye. "With strawberries?"

"If that's what you want." She turned to Shannon. "Dinner's at six. You don't have to bring him if you don't want to."

"Oh, now I'm hurt," Nick said.

With just more than an hour until dinner, Beverly dashed home to prepare and Nick headed back to the school to lock everything down. Shannon rushed back to her motel room, the idea for a new book burning in her head.

High-school homecomings. There were surely as many different customs as there were schools that celebrated the annual event. There would be regional differences. Bound to be. Cowboy Day, for one, wouldn't be a biggie in New Jersey, where she'd gone to school.

Back in her room, she booted up her laptop

and started making notes, things she'd seen, ideas that came to mind. She'd been at it maybe five minutes when someone pounded on her door.

"Go away," she muttered while she finished typing a thought.

Bang bang bang. "Shannon?"

"What?" She sat up and blinked. What was Nick doing here so early?

A glance at the clock beside the bed told her he wasn't early at all. She'd been hunched over her keyboard longer than she'd realized.

"Coming!" she yelled toward the door.

A quick glance in the mirror, a dash of fingers through her hair. She could put on lipstick in a minute. She opened the door and there he stood, looking so good she wanted to lap him up. She reached for him, then clenched her fists and stepped back. "We don't have time."

Nick stepped inside her room and kicked the door shut behind him. "You keep looking at me like that, saying things like that, dinner can wait." He slipped his arms around her and brought his mouth to hers, and she melted against him. "Oh, yeah," he mumbled against her lips. "It can wait a long, long time."

She kissed him back and reveled in the feel of his heart pounding against hers. One of them needed to be sensible, yet when he spread his hand on her backside and flexed his fingers, she doubted it would be her.

Then again, he didn't seem inclined to stop.

She tore her lips free of his and swore. "Why do I have to be the sensible one?"

"Who says you have to be?" He nibbled along the side of her neck.

"Cut that out. Your aunt's waiting for us."

"Oh." He straightened, stepped back. "Yeah. My aunt. Another minute with you and I might forget I even have an aunt. You pack a punch."

"So do you." She held out a hand to ward him off. "So let's not do that again." Lipstick. She needed lipstick. That would keep his mouth off hers. Which wasn't what she wanted, but under the circumstances, Aunt Beverly, dinner. Lasagna. "You or cheesecake? Sorry, you lose."

"My heart would be broken, but I'm after the lasagna."

Shannon shook herself in hopes of regaining her common sense. She swiped lipstick across her lips, fluffed her hair again, then shut down her computer and put it in the bedside drawer.

"Okay, I'm ready." They stepped out of the room. "Are we walking?"

"If you don't mind," he said.

"Are you kidding? I'm from New York, remember? I'm used to walking several miles a day. But I notice nobody walks anywhere around here, except you."

"And one other transplanted New Yorker."

"Wade Harrison?" she asked.

"How'd you know?"

"I recognized the name of the newspaper and remembered that this is where he made off to last summer. What a stir that caused back home, let me tell you."

"I'll bet. Caused quite a stir here, too."

Shannon laughed. "I can only imagine." She hefted her purse strap onto her shoulder and strolled beside him.

"It's something I'll never again take for granted," Nick told her.

"What is?"

"Oh. Sorry. Walking."

"I remember. You were injured. They said you wouldn't walk again. Now you're a walking miracle. Pun intended."

"Pun accepted. It is a miracle, and I don't take it for granted. Or at least I try not to."

"Is that why you walk everywhere? So you won't take it for granted?"

"I walk because if I don't, my back and hip and leg stiffen up."

"But don't you get tired from all the walking? You're on your feet all day, aren't you?"

"I'm on my feet, and yeah, my busted parts get tired and I start limping. I have to walk out the pain before I pack it in for the day, or I'll be sore as hell the next morning."

"Is that your physical therapy? Do you still see a doctor about your injuries?"

"No. They might tell me I'll never walk again, and I'd rather not know that."

Shannon shuddered. "I don't blame you. That must have been terrifying. All of it, from the accident to the prognosis and physical therapy."

"You won't get an argument from me," Nick told her.

"But you did it," she said with quiet awe. "You did it all and survived. Let's celebrate with lasagna and cheesecake."

Beverly Watson and Nick lived two blocks off Main in a small, two bedroom brick house with a neat front yard, with purple and yellow pansies decorating the edge of the sidewalk and front porch. Inside, the house was warm and welcoming, as was the hostess.

"So, you decided to bring him after all."

Shannon shrugged. "He said he was hungry. What could I do?"

"Guess I know where I stand," Nick muttered.

"That's right," his aunt told him. "Why don't you pour the tea, dear, while I finish the salad?" She kissed his cheek.

"Yes, ma'am."

Shannon followed them to the kitchen with an offer of help, and within minutes they were all seated around the oval table in the dining room. The smell of lasagna made Shannon's mouth water.

They talked of this and that, critiqued the parade, considered the upcoming bonfire, which Shannon made Nick promise to take her to see later that evening.

"This lasagna is wonderful, Mrs. Watson."

"Thank you. I knew you had good taste." She smiled and almost winked. "And it's Beverly, please."

"Beverly," Shannon acknowledged. "And I hear your cheesecake is worth…quite a bit."

Under the table, Nick's foot tapped her shin.

"Nick has a weakness for it. Tell me what you do when you're not writing this book you're working on."

"I work for the *Times*."

"The *New York Times?*"

"Is there any other?"

"Spoken like a typical New Yorker," Beverly said with a chuckle. "You write for them?"

"Yes," Shannon said.

"I can't believe," Beverly said, "that a smart, pretty young lady like yourself hasn't managed to convince my nephew to let you interview him yet."

"I can't believe it, either," Shannon said with a look to Nick.

"Does the *Times* know you're writing a book?" Nick asked.

"Yes. They're fine with it. You want to be included?"

"Oho," he said. "You sure slipped that right in there, didn't you?"

She shrugged and smiled. "Seemed like an opportunity too good to pass up."

"You're wasting your breath," he told her.

"Come on, Nick," Beverly said. "Think about it."

"You know I don't go in for that kind of thing," he told her.

Beverly waved a hand in the air as if waving away his words. To Shannon she said, "Those photographers, they violated his privacy time and again, taking pictures of him when he was so hurt he couldn't move. He told them to go away, but they didn't. They had him at what he thought was his worst all over the papers and on television. It wasn't his worst, it was the bravest thing in the world, but that's beside the point. They should have left him alone."

"I agree," Shannon said. "I'm not like that. You know I'm not."

He nodded, giving her the point.

"In their defense," she offered, "you were such big news because you actually saved several lives that they could point to. There wasn't too much of that that day. There was some, but not much. You and the men you saved were individuals they could point to, so they did. Doesn't help you any, but that's what they were thinking at the time."

"You're right," Nick said. "It doesn't help

any. A lot of people died that day. You said yourself that you have firsthand knowledge of that."

"Did you lose someone there?" Bev asked.

Shannon nodded, feeling the old bitter-sweet ache flood through her. "My father."

"Oh, dear." Bev reached across the table and placed her hand over Shannon's. "I'm so sorry."

"Thank you. He was a cop." The words made her heart ache, but she spoke them anyway, as a tribute to her father. "He was pulled from the rubble that first day, but he was already dead."

It was quiet for a moment while they all ate a few more bites and let the ghost of Shannon's father drift away.

"What are you writing about the other people you're including in your book?" Beverly asked.

"Whatever they tell me about themselves. How they have or haven't changed since 9/11. What that day and their part in it has cost them. Their families."

"Maybe you should show Nick what you've written so far. Maybe it would convince him you'll be careful with his story, treat him with respect."

Shannon thought for a moment, thought hard. She normally didn't allow anyone to see her work until it was as clean and polished as she could make it. No eyes on her rough drafts but her own. But she had three chapters she could let him look at that were polished. "Sure," she said. "Will you read some of my manuscript, see what I'm doing? Then, if you still don't want to take part, I'll back off."

Nick was surprised. She must have been

pretty sure of his reaction to extend such an offer. Or she didn't care who read her work-in-progress. "I might do that." It didn't mean he had to give in and be interviewed.

"Okay," Shannon said. "You'll read what I've done on two or three guys and see what you think. I'm only out to tell your story, Nick, not to expose you or make fun of you. Or make you into something you're not."

He nodded once. "Okay. We'll see."

Beverly clapped her hands. "Oh, goody. This calls for cheesecake."

"Don't get your hopes up," he told his aunt darkly.

That was the problem, Shannon thought. Her own hopes were up, and not only about the book.

For the teenagers, the Thursday night bonfire was the highlight of the day, not counting the parade, of course. Someone had gathered what looked like a huge pile of brush, tree limbs and logs in an open field beyond the high school. At dusk, under the watchful yet discreet eyes of police, firemen, teachers and a few parents, the brush pile was set ablaze amid cheers and shouts and laughter. Spirits were high. The cheerleaders led their classmates in several cheers to ratchet up the enthusiasm.

The bonfire was huge. Shannon glanced at Nick and saw him staring at it with narrow eyes. Intense. His jaw flexed. Nose flaring as he drew in the scent of the smoke. Now and then his gaze darted toward one of the firemen, then back to the flames.

What must it be like for him to watch a fire?

"I can't tell," she said, leaning close so he could hear her over the roar of the crowd and the fire, "if that look on your face means you want to watch it burn, or rush in and put it out."

He shook his head and looked down into her eyes. "Neither. Just looking, that's all."

"Uh-huh. Neither? I bet it's more like both. I read somewhere that more than half of all firefighters started out as budding arsonists in their childhood."

He pursed his lips. "Is that a fact?"

"That's what they say," she offered nonchalantly. "Is it true?"

"I don't know," he said. "It's your fact."

She elbowed him in the ribs. "Which half do you fall in?"

"What?" he objected. "You think I started fires as a kid?"

She laughed. "Did you?"

"I can't believe you're asking."

"You're not answering. What did you like to burn?"

"Come on, Malloy, I didn't burn anything." His gaze darted around to make sure no one was listening, then over to that same fireman again. "Much."

"Aha. I knew it. What kind of fires did you start?"

He shrugged and gave her an aw-shucks look. "It was only the trash barrel. And maybe there was the Christmas tree one year. But in my own defense, I was only six, so it doesn't really count."

"I knew it. A budding arsonist. I'll bet your brother was, too. Am I right?"

The instant she mentioned his brother, some of the light went out of his eyes. Shannon could have kicked herself.

"Vinnie?" Even his voice had lost much of

its playfulness and took on a tone of longing that squeezed her heart. "Naw, he was the other fifty percent."

Shannon rubbed his arm and bumped her head against his shoulder in a show of affection and support. For a moment, he let her. "I'm sorry," she said. "Is it still painful to talk about your brother, your dad?"

"Is it painful for you to talk about your dad?" he asked. "He died the same day, in the same way."

"It's a warm ache now," she said. "I'll miss him until the day I die. I'll always hate fanatics who try to force their will on other people, but I'll always be proud of my father. He loved his job and died doing it."

He nodded. "Same here, with my dad and Vinnie."

She waited, but he said nothing more, yet

there was more; it was in his eyes. "But?" she prompted.

He straightened and his face changed. Gone was the brooding look. He was in the here and now, looking as if he didn't have a care in the world. As if he'd never had a love-hate relationship with fire. As if the huge blaze reaching up into the night sky had never held his gaze, never mesmerized him. As if he'd never lost his brother and his father in the flames and explosions, as if he had never had his body crushed that same day.

"But nothing," he said. "You pegged it." He was just a man now, watching teenagers have fun.

Oh, how she wanted a crowbar so she could pry those balled up emotions out of him.

Through their talk and her musings, Nick

had kept visual tabs on that one fireman, the one by the fire truck. Every so often, the man looked back.

"Who is that?" she asked.

"Who is who?

"Would you stop that? You know exactly who I mean. You've been watching that one fireman since we got here like you expect *him* to burst into flames. Who is he?"

"I've never met him."

"Oh, come on. In a town this size?"

"No, really. I guess he's the new fire chief they hired a couple of weeks ago."

"Hired? I thought all the firefighters here were volunteers."

"All but the chief. Somebody got smart about thirty years ago during the oil boom and established several different trust funds with city money. One of the funds was for the fire department. They can pay for a fire chief with experience, thanks to that fund. Everyone else is a volunteer."

"Why didn't they hire you? You've certainly got the experience, and there are no high rises here, so no more than one flight of stairs, if that, per fire. You're more than capable for the job, aren't you?"

He opened his mouth to reply, then closed it and shook his head. "Do you mind if we don't talk about it right now?"

Shannon winced inwardly. She'd been interviewing him. "Sorry. Bad habit. What can I say? I'm naturally curious, especially about people I like."

His grin came quick. "Thanks. I like you, too."

"There you have it. We like each other. We're actually in agreement on something."

"Don't get cocky," he warned, his eyes filled with sudden laughter. "The night is young."

Shannon sighed and watched him resume scanning the crowd and the fire and the new fire chief. Was he warning her with his "the night is young" comment that they weren't going to agree for long? That he was still prepared to deny her the interview even after he read her manuscript? Or was she making too much of a bit of humor?

She looked around and tried to step into the everyday with him and forget his cares, her own cares, for while. It was a beautiful night and she was with the one man in all the world she wanted to be with.

Several people, children and adults, waved at Nick, others called his name and he waved back or nodded.

"Why are so many adults here?" Shannon

asked. "I understand the firemen, but cops? Teachers? Parents?"

"What can I say? It's a small town. Not much else to do, plus, most of the adults went to school here. It's homecoming for them, too. They like to relive their youth."

"And this way it keeps the beer drinking to a minimum?"

"We hope," he said sardonically.

"How about you?" She rubbed her arm against his.

"I'm old enough to drink beer if I want."

"Not that." She pinched his arm. "I mean, do you like to relive your youth?"

He looked down at her. His nostrils flared. "I'm feeling younger by the minute."

An intense look passed between them, and a heat that had nothing to do with the nearby bonfire.

"Oh, look," he said loudly, breaking the moment. "It's the guys. You remember the Three Stooges, don't you?"

It was the three boys she'd met the other day. If memory served, and hers was pretty good, they were Tim, Bosco and Ricky. The minute Nick called them the Three Stooges, they went into a poking and slapping and making-funny-noises routine that they had honed to a fine art. It was pretty funny, she had to admit as she laughed.

"Don't laugh," Nick complained. "It only encourages them."

"Aw, come on, Nick," Ricky said. "You know you like us."

"I *like* Ms. Malloy." Nick slipped an arm around Shannon's shoulders and pulled her to his side. "I *like* fast cars and barbecued ribs. *You* guys, I tolerate. Sometimes. Although I don't know why."

"Because we're cool, man." Tim gripped Ricky's nose between his index and middle knuckles and pretended to twist.

Ricky crossed his eyes while Bosco made silly, Three Stooges–like noises.

"Oh, yeah." Nick nodded his head as if deep in thought. "You three are going to go far in life. With all the attention you give your classes, I wouldn't be surprised to see one of you end up in the White House. Sweeping the floors."

"What the heck, Nick, that's what you do. At least we'd be doing it in the White House."

"What a thing to aspire to. Do you think when I was a kid I used to want to grow up to be a custodian?"

Shannon saw curiosity come into their eyes. "Well, not really," Bosco said.

"What did you want to be?" Ricky asked.

"If you didn't want to do it, how'd you end up here?"

Shannon felt Nick's muscles tighten where he touched her.

"If I wanted to tell you my life story," he said with a cocky grin, "I'd write a book. Then if you wanted to know, you'd have to brush up on your reading skills."

"Hey, man, we read just fine."

"Glad to hear it."

"Look." Bosco nudged the other two boys. "There goes sweet Melissa Sweet."

Tim put his hand up under his shirt and patted his ribs to mimic his heart jumping out of his chest. Ricky threw his head back and howled.

The three of them trailed after the girl like puppies on a leash.

"Come on." Nick turned Shannon away

from the bonfire and the shouting and laughing and cheering kids. "Why don't we get out of here?"

"Sounds fine to me."

She said nothing as Nick took one last look over his shoulder at the bonfire, the flames still leaping up to touch the night sky.

Chapter Six

Away from the light of the fire, it was full dark, broken only by the occasional streetlight or car. Overhead, a million stars blanketed the sky. "Look," Shannon said, tilting her head back. "I've never seen so many stars before."

"I'm almost used to them by now," Nick said, his arm still around her shoulders. "No big city lights out here."

"It's so...breathtaking. I'm a writer. I should be able to think of a better word. Awe inspiring. When I look up I feel insignificant and small. Yet, at the same time, I feel...powerful."

As he watched Shannon, felt her body move beside him, Nick felt the rest of his blood rush straight for his groin. Where most of it had been since she'd first touched him at the bonfire.

He supposed he ought to act like the big he-man, indifferent, aloof. The truth was, he felt too damn good to act any way other than what he felt like—an oversexed teenager. How undignified. Been there. Done that. Thanking his lucky stars he was feeling it again.

"What are you thinking?" she asked.

Nick nearly stumbled on the sidewalk, wondering if he'd spoken aloud. "What do you mean?"

"Just now. You had a grin on your face that would have put the proverbial Cheshire cat to shame."

He grinned again. "I did?"

"Do you always have to answer a question with a question?"

"Do I?"

She raised a fist and gave him a growl.

He laughed again. "I was just thinking that I'd like to race you to the motel, but I'd only humiliate myself when my hip gave out." And then he drew to a halt.

Shannon stopped beside him. "Oh, I don't know. It didn't seem to slow you down any last night."

But he wasn't looking at her. His arm slipped off her shoulders and hung limply at his side while tension stretched his face taut.

"Nick? What's wrong? Is it your hip?"

He blinked and turned his head, looking more than a little dazed. "What?"

"Your hip. You were just talking about your hip, then all of a sudden you stopped and got an odd look on your face. I thought maybe you'd stepped wrong or something and it was hurting."

"No." He blinked and the dazed look faded from his eyes. "Yes. I mean, I didn't hurt it. I made a joke."

"You did, yes."

"About my hip."

"Okay. And that means…?"

A huge smile lit his face and he swooped down and gave her a quick but thorough kiss.

A car zoomed by, going much faster than the twenty-five miles-per-hour speed limit. The radio blared, the occupants yelled and whistled.

"It means," he told her, ignoring the teenagers in the car, "that I may just hang on to you. That's the first time I ever joked about my hip."

"No, it's not," she said. "I've heard you say things about it before."

"Maybe, but I wasn't joking," he said thoughtfully. "This time I was laughing at myself, and I wasn't being sarcastic. Never mind." He slid his arm around her shoulders again and started them back on their way to the Tribute Inn.

"Not never mind." She drew him to a stop. "This sounds to me like a major milestone for you. I think we should celebrate."

"That's what I was planning." He grinned. "That's why we're headed for your room."

"I don't even have a bottle of wine for the occasion," she protested.

"If you did," he said, taking her hand this

time and tugging her down the sidewalk, "you'd have to drink it all yourself, since I don't drink."

"You don't drink? I thought all firefighters at least drank beer."

"Ah, but I'm not a firefighter any longer, am I." He wasn't asking, merely stating fact. "I'm not quite ready to joke about that, so let's change the subject. What did you think of our little bonfire?"

"I thought it was fun. We didn't have a bonfire, or a parade, either, that I can remember."

"You're not really going to write about it, are you?"

"Hmm, maybe, maybe not."

"That's definitive."

"That's all I know. I'm kicking an idea around."

"Maybe I'm better off not knowing," he said. "Although, you wouldn't need to interview me for that one, so maybe I should be encouraging you."

"Lame, Carlucci. Real lame."

"You can't say that to a guy with a bad hip."

"Sorry. No pun intended. But you made a joke about it, so you can't get any more sympathy out of me on that one. You'll have to try something else."

They crossed the motel parking lot and started up the metal-and-concrete stairs.

"Sympathy is not what I want from you," Nick told her.

"Oh, good." She smiled and batted her eyes. This time she managed the key just fine and let them into her room. "Because I've got something else in mind."

"Good." Nick slipped the chain on the door

and turned the knob for the dead bolt. Then he moved toward her, his eyes hot, his lids half lowered. "So do I."

Shannon nearly melted on the spot, and he wasn't even touching her yet. When he did, she would quite likely go up in flames. And she wanted him to touch her. Holding his gaze, she kicked off her shoes and backed toward the bed.

For every step she took, Nick took one toward her. That was a come-hither look in her eyes if he'd ever seen one, and he sure didn't want to disappoint her. One step. Two shirt buttons. Another step. Two more buttons. By the time he stood before her and she had no more room to back up, his shirt lay carelessly across the chair before the window; her sweater decorated the far corner of the bed.

He couldn't wait. He had to taste her. So he did.

He knew he'd promised to read her work, but this, he thought, tasting her mouth, feeling her skin, this was more important. It was inevitable. Unstoppable. What he read of her work might interfere, so this would come first.

Hands tugged and pulled, and clothes dropped to the floor. Shannon took Nick's hand and pulled him down onto the bed with her. "I've been waiting all day for this."

Nick shuddered with anticipation. "Your wait is over."

"Promises, promises."

One kiss, two, and breath turned harsh as lungs demanded more air. Muscles tensed, nerves tingled. Skin turned slick with perspiration. Lips led the way for teeth to nip, hers down his neck, his on the underside of her breasts.

Then he took one nipple into his mouth and suckled, and Shannon's back arched off the bed. A cry of sheer pleasure escaped her throat and shot straight to his loins.

He'd had in mind to go slowly, make it last. Next time. Maybe.

He fumbled for his wallet, but when he pulled out the condom, she took it from him. "Let me," she said breathlessly.

Nick nearly groaned. He didn't know if he could take it, but he gritted his teeth and let her push him over onto his back.

Shannon moved his hands so they rested beside his head, then tore open the packet and straddled his thighs. Looking down and seeing him totally at her mercy gave her a rush of power that was heady in its intensity. Odd that she would feel it so much. She usually didn't feel a lack of power. But then, she didn't usually have a naked man beneath her, hers to do with as she would.

Slowly, one fraction of an inch at a time, she rolled the condom down onto his erection.

"You're about to kill me," he said through clenched teeth.

Shannon smiled slowly. "Is that so?"

He reached for her.

She stopped with the condom only half on and pushed his hands back down beside the pillow again. She gave them a little pat for good measure.

Nick's eyes narrowed. "You'll be sorry when things come to an end way too soon."

She finished with the condom and took him in her hand.

He sucked in a sharp breath, but kept his hands—they were fists now—beside his head.

"As far as I'm concerned..." She positioned herself, then slid down onto him, impaling herself on all that glorious, hard length. "There is no such thing as too soon."

Leaning forward to clasp his fists in her hands, she began to move.

He groaned as if in pain. Even his face looked pained, and she imagined hers did, as well. But it wasn't pain, it was the most exquisite, torturous pleasure, and it demanded more movement, and more.

Soon his hands were on her hips, gripping her tightly, helping her move faster, harder. She rode him, throwing her head back, pulling his hands up to cup her breasts, squeezing him with her thighs, harder, faster, hotter, until the sun burst inside her mind and the world flew away, and she was whole.

An instant later, she felt him follow.

Shannon was the first to speak several long moments later. "Are we still alive?"

"I'm not." Nick relished the feel of her bare back beneath his hands. And her thighs still clamped loosely around his hips. And her hair tickling his nose. "I've died and gone to heaven."

"Mmm. That was a good one." She nuzzled her nose against his neck. "You get points for that."

"Oh, yeah? How many points do I have?"

Against her will, but knowing it couldn't be helped, Shannon eased herself off him and rolled to lie at his side. "Three zillion twenty-two billion ninety-seven million eight hundred fifty-six thousand one hundred."

"Is that all?"

"And four."

"Four? What's the four for?"

She stretched and flung one arm and a leg over him, nestling her head into his shoulder. "For looking sexy dressed as a nerd."

He pinched her gently on her left hind cheek. "You never saw me dressed like a nerd."

"No," she admitted, her eyes closed and a wide grin on her face. "But I pictured it. Black-rimmed glasses, plastic pocket protector. Maybe with the local garage mechanic's logo on it. Half a dozen pens and pencils in there. Maybe a snaggle tooth. Got me hot."

Nick groaned and laughed. "If that's all it takes to get you hot, and if what we just did is the result of said hotness, I'll be hunting up my glasses and pocket protector to wear every day."

"Naw, don't bother." Her energy was bouncing back. She sat up and smirked down at him. "I think the only reason it got me so hot was because I was sitting with you at your aunt's dinner table when the vision hit me. Probably wouldn't have the same effect in person. But you could try it and see. Although, I have to admit, this look works for me." She ran a hand from his shoulder down his torso, his thigh, his leg.

"Much as I hate to admit it," he said, "you're going to have to give me a few more minutes."

"Me, too." She bounced out of bed and disappeared into the bathroom. A minute later he heard the shower running and got up and joined her.

Shannon looked him up and down and laughed. "A few more minutes, my aunt Fanny."

"If you want to read the next chapter, click this tab and the file will open. Don't forget to—"

"I've got it, I've got it."

Nick had pursed his lips and refused to comment when she had opened the bedside drawer a few minutes ago and retrieved her notebook computer from beneath the Bible. She had him set up with it now at the small round table across from the door.

"Believe it or not," he told her, "I have seen a computer before. They have them in Texas. Now, go away and don't look over my shoulder while I read."

"Okay, okay. Sheesh." But she backed

away because she had been acting like a mother sending her first child off to school for the first time. Alone.

Then there was that other emotion zipping through her. She tossed his shirt at him. "If you don't want me hanging around, put that on."

He grinned and gave her an arched look from the corner of his eye. "Is that your way of telling me I'm irresistible?"

She grinned back. "I'm not saying another word. I'm going to finish drying my hair."

As she turned her back and walked away, she heard him chuckle.

She didn't want to see his face as he read. She wasn't in the habit of letting anyone read her work until she turned it in to her editor.

Not that she was in the habit of writing books. This was, in fact, her first. But she never let anyone read one of her articles until she was finished and satisfied with it.

To be fair, she was probably finished with the two chapters she had offered to let Nick read. She'd been over them and over them, and planned to give them only one final read. At some point she had to stop editing and call it done.

Other chapters weren't so polished. Those, she wouldn't let even her mother or Deedra read, much less Nick. And she wasn't trying to impress her mother or Deedra.

Did that mean she was trying to impress Nick?

Of course she was, she admitted, working a dab of styling gel into her shoulder-length hair. She wanted him to like her work so he would let her interview him, so he would want to be included in the project and have a chapter about himself.

Frankly, she just flat out wanted him to like her. Nothing wrong with that, was there?

Then there was the other. The sharp physical attraction.

Call it what it is, Shannon—red-hot sex.

She couldn't deny their attraction, but what made her nervous was that she greatly feared she had overestimated her ability to keep business and pleasure separate. They weren't separate when the man was the same for both. She wanted to interview Nick, and she wanted sex with him. If somewhere in the back of her mind she wanted more than that—if she wanted to be close to him and let their togetherness chase away her loneliness—well, that was her problem, not his. If she wanted more time with him—weeks, months—it wasn't going to happen. She had to go home. She had a life she wasn't willing to give up for anyone, not even Nick.

Not that he had asked her to give up her life and stay with him. Ha! That would be the day.

On the other hand, if she was going to write books instead of articles for the *Times,* she didn't have to live in New York. She could write anywhere, couldn't she? Tribute was a nice little town, friendly, clean.

"Oh, no, you don't."

The sound of her own voice echoing in the bathroom made her jump.

"Did you say something?" Nick called.

She couldn't even turn around and face him. Not with what she'd just been thinking still bouncing around in her head. "No."

"Are you sure? I could have sworn I heard you say something."

"Just talking to myself."

She finally worked up the nerve to peek

over her shoulder and found him hunched over her laptop, his brow furrowed in concentration.

She swallowed. What did that look mean? Did he like what he was reading? Did he hate it? Was he going to let her interview him or tell her to get lost?

She turned on her hair dryer, praying her new gel lived up to its promise.

Before coming to Tribute, she had already decided that if she didn't find Nick, or if he wouldn't cooperate, she would still include him in the book, but in the "Oh, and by the way" chapter where she discussed the rescue workers she hadn't been able to reach.

He wouldn't like that. Neither would she, although for different reasons. He wouldn't like being included at all, if he decided against the interview, whereas she wouldn't like relegating him to the catchall chapter. She wanted to do a full chapter on him.

She turned off the dryer and finger-combed her hair. What was taking him so long out there?

Nick stared at the words on the screen thoughtfully. Knowing Shannon as he did, he didn't know why he was surprised to realize that she was doing something worthwhile with her book. It wasn't sensationalist tabloid journalism, as he had feared, before he'd known her. It was a thoughtful, thought-provoking look at the downstream effects of 9/11 on various individual rescue workers.

She didn't make them come across like sappy fools. They were real. They suffered, they made progress, they lost ground. They were ordinary people who faced a horrendous task and suffered horrendously for it. Some learned to cope better than others. Each person had to figure out for him- or herself the best way to live with the nightmares, the flashbacks, the overwhelming grief.

He wasn't alone. He hadn't given it much thought before, but he wasn't alone. Hundreds of other men and women were fighting the same daily battles he did.

Did that make it any better? Did it ease something inside him?

He thought about it for a long moment and decided that yes, yes it did, in some small way.

That didn't mean he was eager to answer Shannon's questions, but the two guys he'd just read about swore that talking about it helped. "What the hell."

"Are you talking to yourself?"

Nick stared at the screen for another

moment, then closed the files and exited the program. Only then did he turn to face her. "All right. What do you want to know?"

Shannon nearly collapsed in relief. "Thank you, Nick." She crossed the room and placed a hand on his shoulder. "I know this is more or less a leap of faith for you, and I truly appreciate the trust you're placing in me."

He grimaced and rubbed the end of his nose. "Is that the best you can do?"

"Oho, you mean you want a proper thank you?"

He wiggled his brows up and down. "That'd be great."

"Fine." She smiled and held out a hand. "Mr. Carlucci, I'd like to take this opportunity to thank you for agreeing to allow me to interview you for the book I'm working on. I promise not to take up too much of your valuable time."

"Ha ha ha." He took her hand, shook it one time, then pulled on it until she ended up in his lap. "Let me give you my version of 'you're welcome.'"

"Remind me," Shannon said lazily, with a satisfied smile on her face, "to never thank you in public."

"This isn't going to end up in your book, is it?"

With her face buried against his shoulder, Shannon couldn't see his expression. Was he serious? Did he actually think she would? She raised her head to look at him, but his eyes were closed. She couldn't tell what he was thinking. "Please tell me you already know the answer to that."

His eyes popped open. "Hey, I was kidding." He rubbed his hand up and down her back. "If I thought you might use this, what we do behind closed doors, I never would have stepped foot behind your closed door. So to speak." He jiggled her with his arm. "It was a joke, Malloy."

Relief swamped her, made her feel weak. "Boy, talk about your role reversal. Two days ago it was me swearing we could keep business and pleasure separated. Now you're joking about doing the opposite."

He shrugged lightly. "I decided to go along with you on the interview, so that's that. When do we get to that part of it? Frankly," he said, scooting up to lean his back against the headboard, and taking her with him, "I can't imagine what else there is for you to ask that we haven't already talked about."

"Oh, I've got all sorts of questions."

He groaned. "I was afraid of that."

"But not tonight," she said.

"A reprieve?"

"I want to go over the notes I made before I came here, see if I need to make any changes. I don't want to overlook anything. And I'd like to do it on more or less neutral ground."

His lips quirked. "You aren't going to question me while we sweat up the sheets?"

"Fat chance. I'm not ashamed to admit that when you and I are sweating up the sheets, as you so romantically put it, I don't have a single functioning brain cell."

"No kidding?"

This time it was her turn to groan. "There goes your ego, expanding to the tenth power."

"That's just about the most complimentary thing a woman's ever said to me."

"That you're egotistical?"

He poked her in the ribs and made her squeal. "That I scramble your brains. Imagine that." His chest swelled. He all but thumped it with his fist. "Smart lady like you, and I scramble your brains. That's pretty good."

"Proud of that, are you?"

"Darn right. And I guess it's only fair to say that you take my breath away."

Shannon felt everything inside her go still. "I do?" Oh, and how pathetic did that sound, like a little girl unsure of her welcome.

"You don't even have to touch me." He ran his thumb along her jaw and leaned toward her. "You don't even have to be near me. All I have to do is think about you and everything inside me goes all funny." His lips hovered just above hers.

She couldn't stand it. She stretched up until she tasted him, his sweet, soft lips. The kiss was long and slow and easy.

"Funny," she whispered against his mouth. "I think I like that. But…" She trailed her hand down his ribs, his belly, his hip and over to his newly aroused flesh. "Oh, this is not at all funny. And may I just say, thank you very much."

Against her lips, he smiled. "Oh, you are so welcome." He rolled them across the bed until she lay beneath him, and he thought, yes. This was how it should be. The two of them, together, loving each other.

He'd never thought about a woman this way before. About how right they were together. About *them.*

Because he knew *they* would never work, could never last, he took his time and lingered over every kiss, every inch of her fine, pale skin. He kissed every freckle.

He loved her scent, fresh from the shower but still uniquely her own fragrance. He loved the softness of her skin and the sharp contrast against his darker, coarser flesh. He loved the little moans she made, and when she murmured his name, his heart twisted a little.

If he had a working brain cell left in his head, he would get up and walk out the door. He was getting way too attached to this woman, and that way lay disaster. He had agreed to the interview, and when that was done she would leave. He feared she would take the best part of him with her. When the sound of his name on her lips made him feel all warm and fuzzy inside, he was in trouble.

But his hands were fisted in her hair and his lips were fused to hers, and every cell in his brain was fried. He wasn't going anywhere except over the edge of the world. With her. He slipped inside and lost himself in her hot, sweet depths. Reality, and brain cells, could wait until tomorrow. Tonight, he belonged to Shannon.

Chapter Seven

Friday was both Spirit Day and Homecoming Day at Tribute High. The halls and classrooms were a blur of red and white. Teachers and students alike were revved up for the football game later that evening. The football team was cocky; the cheerleaders giggled whenever they saw one another; and anyone who made it from one end of the hall to the other without getting a pom-pom in the face was one lucky individual. Nick had been "accidentally" assaulted twice so far, and there was more than an hour left before classes let out.

Nick tried to remember if he'd ever been as excited over anything as these kids were. Two occasions came to mind: Christmas morning as a kid, and his first day with the Fire Department of New York.

That old association with FDNY had reached out and tapped him on the shoulder when he'd been walking home from Shannon's in the wee hours of the morning. It happened every year the night of the bonfire. Somehow, without planning it, Nick always ended up walking past the remains of the fire after everyone had gone home, just to check. To make sure there were no glowing embers ready to flare up again if given half a chance, like a puff of wind, a dry twig, a piece of paper.

He'd never found a problem on his little walk-bys. The fire department might be mostly volunteer, but they were no slouches. He'd seen them in action and they knew the job. They stared into the belly of the beast, walked into it when necessary. They saved lives, saved property. They had no trouble dousing a bonfire. He just couldn't stop himself from checking.

He didn't usually think about fires, about fighting them. He refused to let himself. That part of his life was over and done with.

But since Shannon had come to town and stirred up old memories—just in time for the bonfire, which didn't help—he felt the old urge rise up in him, the urge to be a part of the brotherhood again, to work along-side his fellow firefighters, to serve the people in his community.

Now he was going to deliberately allow Shannon to poke at old wounds. Man, when she left town, he was going to have to pick up the pieces and put himself back together again. He might have to warn Aunt Bev to keep a close eye on him so he didn't dive back into the nearest bottle. He didn't trust himself to stay sober on his own. Not with all those memories stirred up and brought out in the open. But he knew he wouldn't drink in front of Aunt Bev. She had watched her grandfather drink himself to death. Even at his lowest, Nick couldn't—wouldn't—put her through anything like that again.

Still, he was so much stronger these days, he might be all right on his own. While old memories still haunted him on occasion, and would again, he hadn't been tempted to drink in a long, long time.

Maybe, but when Shannon leaves town, what are you gonna do, pal?

He was going to do nothing, he told himself. Go on with his life. She was terrific. A blast to be with, smart, funny, generous in bed and out. But he'd known from the start that she was temporary. He hadn't even liked her at the start, he remembered with a silent laugh.

And would you look at that mess. Some idiot had obviously shaken a warm cola before opening it. Nice brown splatter decorated half a dozen light tan lockers and a good stretch of the floor before them. Syrupy. Sticky. Great.

Kids. The bane—and, okay, the delight, sometimes—of his existence.

If he wanted something to keep his mind off Shannon—both the lover of the night before and the reporter meeting him at Dixie's after school—scrubbing lockers was as good as anything. Toilets, now, that would do it.

Shannon got to Dixie's Diner ahead of Nick on purpose. It was neutral territory, but she wanted to make the space her own as much as possible. She felt the need for any advantage she could find for her interview with Nick.

The diner was filling up rapidly with people dressed in red and white, as she was, wanting to eat before the big football game at seven this evening. She suspected that nearly everyone in town would be at the game. Nick had asked her to go with him and she was looking forward to it.

It was the interview that had her on edge.

It was silly, the damp palms, the slight tremor in her hands. She had interviewed countless people in her job. She knew Nick in a way she hadn't known any of them. That should make this process easier, shouldn't it?

Yet her stomach was jumping around like a tap-dancing Chihuahua on a caffeine overdose.

Oh, good grief, now I'm starting to sound like I'm from Texas.

Okay, she could still laugh at herself. That was good. She wanted to do this interview. She *wanted* to write about Nick, about what he'd been through, how he'd come to be where he was now. Anticipation, that's what she was feeling. Nothing more. Except raw nerves over what he might think of the questions she asked. Would he think she was silly, trivial? Too intrusive? Should she care what he thought?

Suck it up, girl. This was an interview. That it was with Nick was going to make it easier, not more difficult. Maybe. But it was business. It had nothing to do with the personal side of their relationship. That was her story, and she was sticking to it.

She was checking the contents of her bag, on the floor beside her chair, for the third time—tape recorder, batteries, notebook, pen, backup pen—when the oddest thing happened. The air around her seemed to change. The quality of it, the sound. They were…different somehow. The air both softer yet nearly vibrating with excitement. The sound sharper, clearer, and at the same time quieter.

She knew, without looking, that Nick was there.

Slowly she straightened in her chair, and

saw him threading his way through the tables toward her. And just like that, her nerves melted away, leaving her calm and warm, and oh so glad to see him. "You made it."

"Yeah, it was rough, what with the cross-town traffic, and the buses running late."

Shannon pursed her lips. "You could have taken the subway. It never runs late."

Nick pulled out the chair across from her when what he wanted to do was round the table and kiss that sweet mouth of hers; but instead, he sat down. "Just my luck, the mass trans workers picked this day to go on strike. But I made it anyway, and on time."

She batted her lashes at him. "My hero."

He felt a little lurch in the vicinity of his heart. What he wouldn't give… But he wasn't hero material. Not anymore. "No," he told her. "Just a man."

"And humble, too."

"That's me."

Dixie arrived with ice water and menus. "Hey, Nick, catching a quick meal before the big game?"

"Looks like. What are you doing here so late? You usually go home by now."

"We're swamped. I thought I'd better stay and help out. Hi," she said to Shannon. "Shannon, isn't it?"

"You've got a good memory. What's good for dinner tonight?"

"Pops made a pot roast this afternoon that'll fall apart on your fork, with a flavor to die for."

"That's for me," Shannon said.

"Me, too," Nick said.

They finished off their order with salads, side dishes and two bottomless glasses of iced tea. Dixie brought the latter quickly, then left them alone.

"Was it a madhouse at the school today?" Shannon asked.

"It always is, but I doubt that's what you came all the way from New York to ask me."

"No. No, it's not. You're ready, then?"

"As I'll ever be."

"Okay. We can get some preliminary questions taken care of before our meal arrives." She reached down into her bag and started pulling out the items she needed. "You don't mind if I record this, do you?"

The cassette recorder surprised him. It probably shouldn't have, Nick admitted. And really, what difference did it make? It was an audiotape, not video. And this was Shannon, not some jackass tabloid reporter.

Still, he had to ask. "This tape is just for you, right? I mean, you're not going to let anyone else have it. I'm not going to hear it on the radio, right?"

She smiled, and it spoke of sadness and perhaps empathy. She placed a hand on his arm. "You really have been stung by the media, haven't you?" She gave his arm a warm squeeze. "The tape is just for me, to use as a backup for my notes and my memory. If it makes you uncomfortable, I won't use it." She picked up the recorder and made as if to put it away.

Nick stopped her. "No, go ahead. Just do this the way you usually do."

She gave a small bark of laughter. "It was too late for that several days ago. However, we'll start with basics. I'm going to ask you all sorts of things that might not end up in the book. But they're things I need to know to get a better picture of who you are, where you were in your life on 9/11, how that affected you and brought you to where you are today. I have your vitals, date of birth, immediate family members, your education. I'd like to start with you telling me why you wanted to become a fireman, and when and where you first knew that was what you wanted. Then I'll want to know how you went about joining FDNY."

"Okay, yeah." He chuckled. "I can give you my entire life before our meal gets here."

"Tell me however much you're comfortable with."

"That would be zip," he said.

"Nick. You agreed. Are you going to back out?"

He huffed out a breath. "No, I'm not going

to back out. Okay. Well. First, I was born, but I guess you figured that out on your own."

Shannon rolled her eyes. "Okay, then," she said, turning on her tape recorder and setting it beside him. She stated her name, his name, the date, time and location. "What made you want to become a firefighter?"

Nick huffed out another breath. "I was probably still in the womb, but I didn't understand about fire and firefighters. When I made that connection, that things burned that shouldn't, and men rushed in to stop it, I was about four, maybe. The truth is, I don't remember a time when I didn't want to be a firefighter. My mother used to say it was genetic. I come from a long line of smoke-eaters. My dad, his dad, my mom's dad and granddad. There never seemed to be any question that Vinnie and I would both join the Fire Department of New York as soon as we could. And we did."

"You never thought of doing anything else?"

"Not of my own free will, no."

"You mean because of your injury on 9/11. We'll get to that. But first, how was it for you, working for FDNY? Was it everything you thought it would be?"

"And then some," he said, getting a faraway look in his eyes. "Growing up, Vinnie and I both hung out at the station house as often as we could, but then Dad got transferred from Brooklyn over to Manhattan. That cut our hanging-out time way down. But we saw and heard enough to know what went on, and we were both ready for it. I guess the thing we didn't get, until we were there, was the bond, you know?"

"The bond?"

"You know, with the guys you work with. We call each other brothers. Except for the lack of blood ties, it's true. Especially when you start fighting fires together. We hadn't understood that part of it."

"That was your only surprise?"

He shrugged. "I guess so."

"You didn't get tired of it, living at the station house so much of the time, getting called out at all hours? All that smoke, the fire, the danger? That didn't get to you? Give you second thoughts?"

"How could it give me second thoughts when it was what I thrived on? As far as I was concerned, fighting fires was the reason I was put on this planet. I loved the job."

Dixie returned with their dinners just then, so Shannon turned off her recorder and put it and her notepad in her bag.

"We didn't get very far," Nick remarked after Dixie left them.

"We'll get to the rest tomorrow, if you can spare me a couple of hours during the day. It's Saturday, so I assume you're off?"

"Mostly. I'll have to spend a few hours at the gym and help the crew with their decorations for the dance."

"Ooh, this roast smells like heaven. Would that be the Homecoming Dance?"

"That would be the one."

"You're decorating."

"No, I'm making sure nobody gets killed falling off a ladder or sticking a finger in a light socket, that sort of thing. I am, however, one of the chaperones."

"Boy, are they in trouble."

"Hey, I'm a good chaperone. It's 'do as I say, not as I do.' Wanna go with me? Be my date?"

"To a high-school dance? You mean it?"

"No, I was joking. Of course I mean it. You can wear your jeans and be right at home. Some of the girls will dress up, some won't. I'll even pick you up in the car."

Shannon did a little shoulder thing that made her look as if she were dancing in her seat. "The car? Wow. I have a date for the Homecoming Dance. Ooh, I can't wait."

"You're making fun of me."

Startled, Shannon stopped her antics. "Nick, no. I was teasing, mostly myself. It sounds like a lot of fun, and I mean that. Honest."

"You don't have to go," he said.

"But I want to," she protested.

Nick hesitated, then said, "Good, then. If you're sure."

"I'm positive. It'll be fun."

He smiled. "If you like high-school dances."

* * *

Nick had never known a woman like Shannon. She had a million different moods, a mind like a steel trap and an outrageous sense of humor. With hair he loved to sink his hands into and a body designed expressly for him. Around her he felt at peace, which was an odd thing to think, since he also felt more excited than he ever had with other women.

Not that he remembered any other women. When he was with Shannon, it seemed as if there weren't any, had never been any.

He had to get this damned interview over and done with so she could go back to New York before he did something completely stupid, like fall in love with her.

But, no, he had to go and invite her to the game tonight. And the dance tomorrow night. That had been a stroke of idiocy. Masochism.

But the thought of holding her in his arms and swaying to some slow, romantic song from the fifties had scrambled his brain.

Sitting next to him in the bleachers, as the band finished its halftime marching number and people were streaming from the stands toward the concession booths, Shannon nudged him. "What are you looking so serious about?"

He made a sound that even to him sounded suspiciously like a grunt. "Uh… nothing. Really."

"O-kay." She said it as if agreeing with a mental patient that yes, of course he had three arms. Very carefully, so as not to upset him.

Nick chuckled. "I was hoping they don't play a lot of rap at the dance tomorrow night."

"You don't like rap?"

He narrowed his eyes. "Do you?"

She narrowed hers. "I asked first."

He shook his head. "Mostly I don't get it."

"Well, that's all right. You're not who they're aiming for, anyway."

He gave her a half smile. "The rap music industry isn't aiming for an audience of old has-beens?"

Shannon tilted her head and studied him. "That's not really how you see yourself, is it?"

"Is that an interview question?"

She groaned and barely stopped herself from stomping her foot. "There you go again, answering a question with a question."

"You answer a question with a complaint."

She laughed at him, and he made a face at her.

"Carlucci, how's it going?"

Shannon nearly swallowed her tongue when she recognized the man who came and sat sideways, facing them, on the next bench down.

"Pretty good. How about yourself?" Nick shook the man's hand.

"No complaints. I'm being nosy. Maybe it's the newspaperman in me, but I believe I know your friend. It's Malloy, isn't it? Shannon Malloy?"

Now she really was speechless. She had met Wade Harrison once five years ago at a *Times* Christmas party. Someone had introduced them and they had shaken hands and talked for maybe fifteen seconds, at most. And he remembered her name?

When she realized both men were staring at her, she jerked and held her hand out. "Mr. Harrison, how are you? I can't believe you remembered me after all this time."

Harrison smiled. "The Christmas party,

right? You had been writing the articles on the city-council scandal of the time. Kick-backs, if I recall."

"That's right." She swallowed. The man was a legend. He was practically royalty in her business. "How are you finding life in a small town?"

"I find it just about perfect," he said. His smile practically beamed when Dixie, the woman from the diner, filed past with two young boys and one old man and waved on their way down the stairs.

"His family," Nick explained to her.

"That," Harrison said with a nod toward Dixie and the boys, "is what keeps me here. What about you? What are you doing so far from Manhattan? Working on a story?"

She shrugged, suddenly shy about talking about her work in front of the former president and CEO of Harrison Corporation, one of the largest, most successful media conglomerates in the country. "A book," she answered.

"Anything to do with our boy, here?" He nodded toward Nick.

She glanced at Nick.

"He knows who I am. Was. Whatever," Nick muttered.

"You told him?"

"Didn't have to," Harrison said. "I recognized him. We recognized each other, actually, and at the time, neither of us wanted our identity revealed."

"Now Nick's the only one denying his past," she said. Then she closed her eyes. "Nick, I'm sorry. I didn't mean that the way it sounded. Your past is your business and I'm not criticizing you for keeping it private. Honest."

"Don't beat yourself up over it," Nick said. "Something tells me I'm about to be outed."

"Not by me," she said honestly. "My book won't be published for more than a year. And I'm certainly not going to mention where you live. If you lived in Manhattan, sure. But not a small town like this so that anyone could find you easily. I'm—"

"I didn't mean you," Nick said, nodding a greeting to someone approaching from behind Shannon.

She turned and glanced over her shoulder. It was the fire chief. The one Nick had been eyeing the night before at the bonfire.

"Hey, Lon," Wade Harrison said. "I assume you know Nick?"

"No, don't believe I've had the pleasure." He held out his hand and Nick shook it.

"Nick Carlucci, meet Lonnie Wallace, our new fire chief."

The chief cocked his head and peered at Nick. "I know you, don't I? Not from here, but from before. Carlucci. New York, right? You were with the FDNY on 9/11. You're the one who saved Barry."

"Barry Cunningham?" Nick asked.

"Yeah. Man, it is really— If I'd realized who you were, I would have introduced myself and told you thank you from my whole family."

Nick looked stunned. Shannon took over the conversation. "Barry Cunningham. He's one of the seven men Nick saved when he got injured, right?"

"That's right. It was all over the news, the way he pushed them out of the way, then took the hit himself when that giant beam collapsed. Barry was one of the seven. He's my cousin's husband. And I'm sorry, I didn't get your name."

"No problem." Shannon shook his hand and introduced herself.

"You're the reporter I've been hearing about," Lon told her.

"Nothing wrong with the grapevine in this town," she said with a laugh.

"You got that right," Nick muttered.

"How is Barry doing these days?" she asked Lon. "Is he having any of the adverse health effects we've been learning about in the news the last couple of years?"

"Oh, no, Barry's doing fine. Thanks to Nick, here."

"No, please," Nick said. "I didn't do much."

"You saved their lives. Hey, guys," he called out. "Come over here and meet the man."

To Nick's credit, Shannon noted, he

barely cringed, but there was no mistaking the resignation in his eyes. His secret was out. She wondered why it had been so important to him to keep his past buried in the first place.

Two young men wearing Tribute Fire Department caps came from the other side of the bleachers. "What's up, boss?"

The fire chief introduced Nick and Shannon to the two young volunteer firefighters, then someone else overheard and stopped by. Within minutes they were surrounded by a knot of people, one of whom was one of Harrison's stringers for the newspaper, who just happened to have his camera with him.

Shannon wondered which one would make the front page of the next issue—homecoming or Nick Carlucci, 9/11 hero.

"I wonder," Lon said to Nick. "Could I impose upon you, Nick, and ask your advice?"

The smile Nick managed was a little weak around the edges, but Shannon doubted anyone but her noticed. "Sure," Nick said. "What about?"

"Well, I guess you've been out of the business a while, but you've still got more experience fighting fires than I do. I mean, I trained up in Wichita Falls and worked there for several years, so I'm no probie, but, well, tomorrow we're scheduled to go over the nursing home and check their escape plans. Maybe see about a fire drill. They've got some new employees over there that I hear aren't up to snuff on emergency procedures. I'm wondering if maybe you might be able to stop by over there tomorrow around ten and give me a pointer or two, see if I'm missing something."

"I doubt I'll be able to tell you anything you don't already know, but I'd be glad to help."

"Great." Relief was visible on Lon's face. He shook hands with Nick again. "Great. Thanks. I really appreciate it. Come on, fellas, let's leave Nick to his date. Ma'am, nice meeting you." He nodded to Nick and to Wade Harrison, then he and his fellow firefighters ambled down the steps.

"I guess he was a little nervous about this inspection tomorrow," Wade said. "It was good of you to agree to help."

Nick gave a small shrug. "I doubt I'll be any help, but I couldn't really say no, could I?"

"Guess not. And now you're outed." Wade stated the obvious. "Even my ace reporter overheard."

Nick winced. "You're not gonna make a big deal out of this in the paper, are you?"

"You saved his cousin's life."

"Yeah? So?"

"So, he thinks it's a big deal. I'll do what I can to keep it as low key as possible," Wade said, "but I won't be able to keep it out of the paper. Sorry, pal, but you're news. Too many people will want to know why the paper never mentioned a New York reporter was in town. The rest will come from there."

When he left, and they were finally alone again, Shannon reached over and took Nick's hand. "I'm sorry you've been outed."

Nick looked down at their joined hands and threaded his fingers through hers. Hers were so delicate, he could probably crush them just by squeezing his together. Yet they held the power of the sword in them, by way of her writing. When she touched him in bed, they held such fire as to render him sense- less. Now, compassion. All of this, just from her delicate hand.

"Don't apologize," he told her. "It had to come out sooner or later. I knew when you came to town people would wonder why a New York reporter wanted to talk to a high- school custodian."

"I'm thinking of a book."

With a wry grin, he looked up from their joined hands to see her staring off into the distance, with that *I'm writing in my head* look in her eyes. "About a high-school cus- todian? That ought to sell about three copies."

"A crime-fighting high-school custodian. He and the students get involved in various capers…. I could write an entire series. Nancy Drew, look out."

"Nancy Drew appeals to girls," he pointed out.

Shannon gave him a long, slow look up and down that had his temperature rising.

"So do some high-school custodians."

Chapter Eight

"You don't have to stay, if you'd rather not," Shannon said, her nerves twisting into tight knots.

Nick tore his attention from the television and looked at her. "You want me to go?"

The Tribute Tigers had won their homecoming game, and after joining the throng for an ice-cream cone at the Dairy Queen, Nick had walked her back to her room. He'd turned on the television and stared at it without saying a word. That was ten minutes ago. He was brooding. She recognized it easily, as her father used to act the same way when something heavy had weighed on his mind. The trick was getting him to unload, or share the burden.

"No, I don't want you to go," she told Nick. "Do you want to talk about it?"

He stared at her, then looked back at the television. "I don't know what you're talking about."

Shannon felt a hot stinging behind her eyes. Her vision blurred. She whirled away from him and closed herself in the bathroom until she could beat back the threatening tears. He had just shut her out completely. They had been as close as a man and woman could be, physically, but he wouldn't talk to her about what had happened at halftime with the fire chief. Nick had lived quietly, anonymously, in this town for more than two years, and now things were going to change. People were going to see him differently, maybe treat him differently. They would ask questions that they thought were innocent but that would cut him to the bone, about what it had been like that September day.

She knew what he would be going through because she'd heard it all a dozen times from other men and women who had been there, done that, and lived to tell the tale.

If there was one thing she knew, silence was Nick's enemy, yet it was the one thing he held on to the hardest.

Well, to hell with that. She flung open the bathroom door and marched over to the television. She couldn't turn it off because Nick had the remote in his hand and she didn't know where the power button was. Searching for it would take something away from the statement she was trying to make, so she stood in front of it, arms folded, and stared at him until he looked her in the eye.

"I was watching that," he protested.

"Oh, really? What is it?"

"What difference does that make?"

"You don't know, do you? You weren't watching anything. You were using the television to stare at so you wouldn't need to talk to me, so you wouldn't have to deal with having had your cover blown tonight."

"My cover blown?" He all but snorted. "That's a good way to put it."

"What do you think will happen when more people find out? How many of the people you know are going to care what you did or didn't do five years ago?"

He stared at her hard, almost glared, for a long moment, chin up, shoulders tensed as if to ward off a blow. Or launch one. Then, he slowly wagged his head back and forth in defeat. His shoulders drooped. "Who knows," he said.

"Come on." He'd made a good start in acknowledging her question. Such a simple thing, but it hadn't been easy for him. She took him by the hand and led him to sit beside her on the bed. "Tell me the worst thing that can happen now, regarding people learning about your past. How bad can it get?"

He looked at her out of one eye. "You're not making fun of me, are you? You're really asking."

"I'm really asking. Let's figure this out," she encouraged. "Maybe make a plan or two to deal with it."

He groaned and rolled his eyes. "You're one of those goal-oriented positive thinkers, are you? Plan your work and work your plan, or some such garbage."

"I see you've found your sense of humor again. That's good. Planning has its place in the overall scheme of things, but I also enjoy flying by the seat of my pants."

He reached out and trailed his hand down her outer thigh. "And a very fine seat it is, pants and all."

"Okay. I'd say you're feeling better."

"Can we just drop it? I'm not giving out any more interviews tonight." He shifted until they lay together, crossways on the bed. He rose above her, his weight braced on one forearm, his hips pressed against hers. "I can think of better things to do."

Shannon smiled and ran a finger across his lips. "I bet you can." She was torn. Give him this easy way out of talking and make love with him, which they both wanted anyway, or push him away and try again to get him to talk about what was uppermost in his mind.

When he buried his mouth against the side of her neck, the question became moot. She could never push this man away. He was too much in her blood. When she tried to think about going home without him, all she could envision was darkness. All she felt was loneliness. Only with Nick was she safe and warm and part of a whole, solid unit. Only with him was she not alone.

* * *

Shannon was the first to recover enough for speech. "If you promise that I never have to move again, I'll worship you forever."

"Okay. If I don't move again, you won't be able to. I know I'm crushing you." He moved his arms as if to push himself up.

Shannon held him close. "No, stay. Please. You're not crushing me."

They lay that way, wrapped in each other's arms, with Shannon reveling in his heat and weight, for a long while. She thought he might have dozed for a bit, but eventually, he rolled aside. It was impossible to feel rejected, for he took her with him and snuggled up against her.

"Better?" he asked.

"Almost perfect."

"Almost? What would make it perfect?"

Shannon pushed herself up onto her elbow and looked at him. "If you would talk to me. I don't mean the interview," she said in a rush when he started to speak. "I mean about what you're facing around town tomorrow."

"Tomorrow." He closed his eyes. "That soon, huh?"

"Hey, wait a minute. It just occurred to me that twice in recent months—once when somebody found out Wade Harrison was here, and again a few weeks later when he dedicated that new monument to his heart donor and then got married—this town has been flooded with media and paparazzi. Every radio and television network, every magazine, every major newspaper. They were all here. How the devil did you avoid being recognized? *Someone* should have known you by sight in that group, surely."

"Wade gave me a heads-up, so I lay low while they were here."

"How do you lay low in a town this size? What did you do, stay home?"

He gave a wry laugh. "The first time, it was summer, so, yeah, I kept pretty close to home. But for the monument and the wedding, I had to be at school every day. We were shorthanded, and I had to spend some time at the elementary school, where Dixie's boys go, so don't think I wasn't worried. But I kept out of everyone's way. Drove instead of walked. If I had to walk, I stuck to back alleys."

Shannon shook her head. "All that trouble, and now here you are, a few weeks later."

"Huh. It's one thing for the town to learn who I am. Most of them won't care. But with that other group, the media and whatnot, I would have been plastered all over the place again. Just like last time."

"Just what did happen with the media? Oh—no. Don't answer that. That's an interview question. We'll get to it tomorrow. Except you've got an appointment tomorrow."

He looked away and stared at the television.

"You do remember, don't you?" she prodded.

"Remember what?"

"You promised to meet the fire chief at the nursing home at ten."

"Oh, that. Yeah, I remember."

"You don't think somebody's going to comment on the fact that you've been a firefighter more years than some of those volunteers have been alive?"

"*Was,*" he said grimly. "*Was* a firefighter. And I'm only thirty-two."

"All right, thirty-two, and *was*. And why—
No, I'm going to save that question. What's
your worst nightmare stemming from
people knowing you're the firefighter who
saved those people? From your being a
hero."

"That." He shot out from beneath her and
jumped from the bed. With jerky movements
he stepped into his jeans, then started pacing
the floor. "That word you used. *That's* my
worst nightmare."

"Well, now. I guess I hit a nerve. I just
wish I knew what word you're talking
about. Do you mean *hero?*"

"Oh, that's the one, all right."

Along with the anger and frustration that
lit his eyes, she thought she detected a hint
of fear. "You have no idea how badly I want
to ask you why that word causes you such a

problem. But I'd rather save that for the interview."

"That figures."

"Don't take that tone with me." She sat up and pulled the sheet up to cover her body. "You knew why I was here from the start. No law says you have to say anything."

"That's right, I don't."

Shannon stiffened. "Are we fighting?" Her eyes popped wide. "I think we're fighting."

"You don't have to sound so excited about it. We've been fighting from the minute you walked up and introduced yourself to me."

"We've been disagreeing, not fighting."

"So what's different now?"

"I don't know." She grinned. "It just seems like, since we're sleeping together, we should be able to fight about something now and then, so we can make up."

He raised his hands in surrender. "All right, let's fight. What about?"

She tightened the sheet over her breasts. "I think we should figure out what you can say to people tomorrow when they ask you about…you know."

Nick flopped down on the chair beside the table. "You're not going to let this go, are you?"

"No." She scooted to the edge of the bed. "Be thinking about it while I get dressed."

"Don't get dressed on my account." There was a cute little whine in his voice that made her laugh.

"Sorry, big guy." But when she came out of the bathroom a few minutes later, she wore panties and an oversize T-shirt.

"Okay, down to business." She plopped onto the bed. "More people are going to know about you by tomorrow. Some of them won't know the details and will ask you about how you saved the men, or about the injury you sustained doing it, or the seriousness of your injury, your miraculous recovery, why you left New York, and why you're not a local firefighter. Anything else?"

"Isn't that enough?" he said, resignation in his voice.

"All right, then. Let's see." She tapped her finger against her cheek and studied the ceiling. She knew where she wanted to lead him, but wasn't quite sure how to get him there. He was a man, after all, so the sensible, direct route would never do.

"What are you thinking?" he asked, suspicion coloring his voice. "You're looking way too innocent for comfort."

"All right, all right. Tell me something. If

everyone you know in town comes up to you tomorrow and calls you a hero, tells you they admire you, asks you all those questions you don't want to deal with—what would happen if, during the next few days, it was as bad as you've imagined it could be? What would happen?"

"What do you mean?"

"What would happen? Would the sky fall?"

"Now you're making fun of me."

"I'm not. I'm asking you to seriously consider what's going to happen tomorrow and the next days and weeks. Will people start to hate you? Will you start to hate them? What?"

Nick scowled. "Of course I'm not going to hate them. Why would I hate them? The main thing I have a problem with is that damn word."

"Hero?"

"That's the one."

"I guess it would be uncomfortable to be called a hero."

"You don't know the half of it," he said heatedly. "People throw that word around and expect you to live up to it. Expect you to be perfect." He shoved up from the chair and started pacing. "Better than perfect. Who can live up to that?"

He threaded his fingers through his hair in agitation. "You're expected to do something heroic every time you turn around. Kitten up a tree on your block? Call the hero, he'll get it down. Backed-up toilet? Why, we've got a hero down the street. He'll take care of it. Then you do something maybe not so heroic, like, oh, I don't know, let the grass get too high, or drink too much, or don't wash the car or paint the house when it needs it. Then, instead of just being a normal person, you're a disappointment to all those people who thought you were a hero and expected you to be perfect and heroic every damn day for the rest of your damn, stinking life."

For once, Shannon was at a loss for words. She didn't know what to say to help him. He was obviously speaking from experience; platitudes would be worse than useless, they would be condescending. "I'm sorry," she said quietly.

He whirled on her. "What for?" The words shot out as if fired from a gun.

"I'm sorry that someone made you think you had to live up to all that. I can see some of the problems it can cause."

"When you try to tell them you're nobody's

hero, just an ordinary man, they argue with you, or think you're being humble or something, or they get hurt or mad because they *need* a hero, and they expect you to be it."

Shannon ached for the anguish he tried to disguise with anger. "Come here."

He narrowed his eyes. "Why?"

"Because I like sitting next to you."

He dropped his head and heaved a sigh. "I'm being an ass, right?"

"No." She scooted back on the bed until she sat against the headboard. Then she patted the space beside her. "That's a pretty heavy load for anyone to carry."

"Yeah?" He hooked his thumbs in the front pockets of his jeans.

Across the room Harry Potter was working on a new spell on one of the cable channels, but the sound was off.

"What happens at the nursing-home inspection you're going to tomorrow?"

He let out a low groan. "Don't remind me."

"Come on, it can't be that bad. This guy's a real firefighter. He's not going to...oh, yeah. You saved his cousin."

He chewed on the inside of his cheek.

"Well, you did. That's a fact. If he thanks you again, just say you're welcome and change the subject."

"You make it sound easy."

"I know. And I imagine it's not easy at all. I don't know what else to say. But what about the inspection? What's going to happen with that?"

"The chief will do most of the talking, and every now and then I'll grunt. That's what we men do when we don't want to say anything, or don't have anything to say."

"For shame. You're going to have to come up with something better than a grunt. This is a fire-safety inspection."

He shrugged. "I don't have the training for that, and I don't know the Texas fire codes."

"But you know what's safe and what's not."

"I guess that's true."

"You're just going there to put in your two cents. Maybe make a recommendation or two that goes beyond what's required and speaks to what's best for the residents of the home."

"Listen to you, Little Miss Crusader." His smile took any sting out of the words.

"Now and then, yes, I tend to climb up on my soap box." She eyed him pointedly. "But I try to keep an open mind about most things."

"Touché." He pulled her close and kissed her.

* * *

Nick felt like a naughty teenager, sneaking into the house along with the first rays of the sun, carrying his shoes so as not to make noise, after a night of hot sex.

"Do you want some breakfast?"

Startled, Nick dropped his shoes. "Damn, Bev, you could give a guy a heart attack sneaking up on him that way."

She stood in the kitchen doorway, arms folded, lips pursed so as not to laugh out loud at him, he was sure.

"I don't believe I'm the one who was sneaking."

Nick felt his face heat up. Great. He was blushing. And he was trying hard not to laugh because, remembering his conversation with Shannon not too many hours ago, he had the overwhelming urge to answer his aunt with a grunt. But he didn't think she'd stand for it. "I was trying not to wake you."

"Nice save. I'm making pancakes."

"Yes, please."

Over breakfast Bev informed him that, after the game last night, she had overheard someone at the pizza parlor talking about Nick the janitor being some "How did he put it? Some big-time 9/11 hero."

This time he did grunt. There wasn't a thing in the world to say about that.

"I guess your secret is out."

"The new fire chief recognized me."

"He's been here for more than two months. Why is he just now recognizing you?"

"I haven't seen him up close except his second day in town when he toured the schools. But I've seen him around lately. Then he found out I'm hanging around with a reporter from New York, and tonight he saw me at the game talking to Wade Harrison, also from New York. He put it together and asked me if I was the guy who saved his cousin when the Twin Towers fell."

"Oh."

Nick nodded and jabbed a huge bite of pancakes into his mouth so he wouldn't have to talk about it anymore.

A futile effort. No way would Aunt Bev let him change the subject. Not when she'd been wanting him to tell the truth about himself for years.

"Are you all right?" she asked gently.

"I'm not thrilled about it all, but I knew the day was coming, sooner rather than later, when Wade Harrison moved to town."

"Wade told?" Her tone and expression

would have been the same if she'd asked if Wade had taken a knife to him.

"No, it wasn't him, but he knew me the first time he saw me, his first week in town, back when he was washing dishes for Dixie, remember?"

Bev smiled. "I remember," she said. "So, you're okay, then?"

"I will be. Don't worry, Bev, I'll be fine. If I make it through today, I'll make it through anything."

"We already know you can survive anything. What's today?"

"Assisting the new fire chief with a fire-safety inspection at the nursing home, and maybe a fire drill. Then I get to hang around the gym and make sure nobody falls off a ladder or shorts out the wiring or anything while they decorate for tonight's dance."

"And then?"

"And then," he said with a smile, "in between breaking up fights, hauling out drunks, and pouring out the punch and starting over as soon as they've spiked it, I get to dance with a sexy lady reporter from New York."

"You like her," Bev noted, sounding satisfied.

"What's not too like? Except that she's a reporter, but nobody's perfect."

But Shannon was as perfect as they came, Nick thought. Perfect for him.

And he wondered, what was a man supposed to do when the woman was the right one, but he was the wrong man for her? She deserved a whole man, not one with huge doubts about himself.

She had helped put him partially back together, and that was the truth. But there was more to being a man than sex. Not that he wasn't grateful to have that part of himself alive and active again. But there was more, and he didn't have it. He'd lost it when that beam had fallen on him, and he didn't know how to get it back. Or if he ever would.

Chapter Nine

The nursing-home inspection was not the ordeal Nick had feared. The inspection team consisted of Lon, a couple of town council members and a representative from the state's fire safety board. And Nick, for whatever that was worth. The owner of the facility was there, as well, and the two staff members designated as fire-safety staffers.

Then, of course, there was the local media. The safety of the nursing-home residents warranted one reporter/photographer from the *Tribute Banner*—and Shannon. She came sidling up to Nick where he stood at the back of the group while the owner gave his spiel about how much he appreciated the city working to make the patients and building safe.

As if she thought Nick didn't realize she had entered the building and was standing beside him—not know? How could he not know when she walked into a room? He could be dead and he would know. Shannon nudged his arm with her shoulder.

"What are you doing here?" he asked, keeping his voice low.

"I'm thinking of an exposé on nursing homes."

"Liar," he whispered.

"Shh. The man's speaking," she whispered back, her eyes twinkling with laughter.

He'd been dreading this event all morning. So much so that, although he hadn't realized it, his stomach had tied itself in knots. The only reason he was aware of that fact now was that when Shannon showed up, his tension eased.

If he bottled her, they could make a million. No more muscle relaxants, antidepressants, heartburn medication, sleeping pills. Just Shannon. With Shannon, everything was all right, and if it wasn't, a man just didn't care.

He was getting way too used to her, way too needy.

But that was a worry for another day and time. Right now she was here beside him, so he could handle whatever they threw his way.

As it turned out, they didn't throw much at

all until after the inspection. The facility wasn't four-star accommodations, and the smell wouldn't win any prizes, but for what it was, it was all right.

"How did they do?" Shannon asked Lon as he finished taking notes.

"Oh, not too bad."

"I noticed on the Internet last night that in a federal GAO 2004 survey report, 1,143 Texas nursing homes responded to the survey, and eighty-four-point-four percent had fire-safety deficiencies. Care to comment?"

Poor Lon, Nick thought. The guy looked like a deer caught in the headlines of an oncoming semi.

"Uh, well, uh, you see…"

"It's a courtesy thing, Shannon. He gets to tell the owner and the officials how they did before it goes to the press."

"That's it." Lon looked at Nick as if he were his new best friend. "That's it exactly."

Meanwhile, the guy from the local paper wore a maniacal grin and scribbled notes like mad.

Lon pulled Nick aside and quietly thanked him. "For a minute there, I thought I was on *60 Minutes* or something. That woman is scary."

Nick just smiled.

"So, what do you think?" Lon motioned to indicate the nursing home in general.

"Well, I wouldn't want to live here, but I've seen worse."

"Ain't it the truth. But they've got some things they need to take care of to bring them up to code. They're going to have to figure out a better way to keep track of their patients than by locking that back door, for one thing. They knew we were coming today and they still had that chain on it."

"So much for his fine talk about what's best for the residents," Nick added.

"Did you see anything worth noting?"

Nick shrugged. "You've got the checklist to work down, so I didn't pay much attention to that. Of course, the first thing they should do is put in a sprinkler system."

"Naturally. But it's not required by law, so they won't. I'm still going to hound them on it, though."

"They can at least put a smoke alarm in every room."

Lon grinned. "Maybe I'll threaten them with your reporter friend if they don't."

"Damn, man, you're just plain mean."

"I try. Hey, listen, thanks, brother."

"No problem," Nick said, shaking the man's hand.

"It's none of my business why you left New York, or why you're not fire chief here. I guess if you were, I wouldn't have a job. But if you ever feel like volunteering, you know we can always use an experienced hand."

"Thanks for the offer." Nick smiled wryly. "I'm out of the business because my leg can't be trusted. If I put too much pressure on it, it gives out. I can't haul pipe up stairs. Hell, I probably couldn't haul it across the room, not in full turnout gear. In New York, if you can't climb stairs, you're useless fighting fires."

"I hear that," Lon said with feeling. "But the offer still stands. You'll notice we don't have a lot of stairs around town. Certainly nothing more than one or two flights. And we have a bunch of strong young guys to haul pipe all day and all night."

"Excuse me." The local newshound had been so quiet, Nick had forgotten him. Now the kid raised his pen for attention. "What is this pipe you talk about hauling?"

"Civilians." Lon rolled his eyes. "That's what we call a fire hose. It's a water pipe. Get it?"

"Oh, yeah. Cool."

Nick and Lon shared a look, and a smile.

"See? Didn't I tell you you had nothing to worry about?"

Nick glanced at Shannon, then back at the pizza menu on the wall. "You did not."

"Are you sure?"

"I'm sure. I'm having the works on my half. What do you want?"

"Everything but anchovies. It went okay,

though, didn't it? Nobody made a big deal out of you or anything? You weren't put on the spot, or asked to reenact breaking your back?"

Nick snickered. "No. It was fine."

When he reached for his wallet—you had to pay when you ordered—Shannon pushed his wallet aside. "This is on me. We're celebrating."

"What are we celebrating?"

"Your successful outing."

The kid behind the cash register, Bucky Jones, who'd graduated from Tribute High last year, nearly swallowed his tongue. "G-g-g-olly, Mr. Nick."

"She didn't mean that the way you think," Nick said darkly. "Shannon, tell Bucky you didn't mean that the way he thinks."

"What? Oh." Shannon laughed. "No. Sorry. It wasn't that kind of outing."

* * *

If Nick hadn't had to spend the afternoon overseeing the decorating at the high-school gym, Shannon could have finished interviewing him. But since their time was short, she decided to put it off until after the dance that night and let him eat his pizza in peace. They had only one small incident during their lunch.

That came when Nick, rather offhandedly, Shannon thought, casually mentioned that he'd been wrong about the jeans for the dance. He'd been told in no uncertain terms that this was a dress-up affair. The Homecoming Queen candidates would be in formal gowns; the rest of the females attending the dance would most likely be in party dresses. "Whatever the hell that means," he added.

Shannon checked her watch. "You're

telling me this…a whole six or seven hours in advance? Why, thank you."

"Sorry," he grumbled. "But we're chaperones, not attendees, so I figure we can wear whatever we want."

"You just go right ahead and figure that. Me? I'm wearing a dress. If you want to be seen with me, wear a sport jacket."

His lips twitched. "Yes, ma'am."

When they left the pizza parlor, Nick and Shannon went their separate ways. He, to help at the gym. She, to make her way back to the motel and work on her notes.

She sat hunched over her laptop for a few hours, transcribing her notes from Nick's interview so far.

She really had only two or three other questions for him. She wanted to hear about his recovery, when he wasn't supposed to recover. About his troubles with the press and media. What did it do to him to realize he couldn't fight fires anymore? Was that why he'd left New York? Why he now pushed a broom for a living? Was he okay with that? Would he ever go back to New York?

She paused over that last question, her heart suddenly thundering in her chest. Because that last question had less to do with her book and more with her personal wishes. She simply couldn't imagine going home and never seeing him again. The mere idea left her cold inside.

When she had first come to town, there had been something in Nick's eyes, or rather, something lacking. She hadn't realized it then, but she did now, because today it was back. It was a holding back, a certain distance he tried to keep between himself and the rest of the world.

But for a few days, he'd been hers. When they'd made love, he had quit holding back and started being open with her, letting her see and feel his vulnerability. He'd let her get emotionally close to him, giving her everything he had. She had felt it in his touch, tasted it in his kiss. Seen it shining in his eyes. He'd been hers.

Even last night, he'd been hers. And he had accepted that she was his. Until today. Like watching someone pull down a window shade, she had seen the shield come down over his eyes at the nursing home, when he'd been reminded firsthand that he would never be a fireman again.

And that was just nonsense, she thought, suddenly fuming. Maybe he couldn't haul pipe up fifty flights of stairs, but there were other things he could do.

Here she'd been, planning on going easy on him during the last of her interviews. She hadn't wanted to push him too hard. Heaven forbid she ask a question that might cause him discomfort.

But she was not going to give up without a fight.

Just what that meant, she didn't know and didn't want to think about. Did she mean her interview? Did she mean getting Nick to see himself as something other than a has-been? Or did she mean something much more personal?

She wouldn't dissect it. She would start with one and work her way toward the others.

But first there was a more immediate problem that had to be solved. What the heck was she going to wear to the Tribute High School homecoming dance?

* * *

A veteran shopper could always find something appropriate to the occasion. Shannon discovered a cute little shop on Main that offered a little bit of everything a young, stylish woman could want, and exactly what Shannon needed for the dance.

She carried her purchase back to the motel. As she was getting out of the shower, her phone rang. It was Deedra.

"Why are you still there? Why haven't you called? It can't take all week to interview one man, and if it does, he's probably not worth it."

"Deedra?"

"You've got other chapters."

"Deedra."

"One guy, I don't care who he is, isn't worth this much of your time."

"Deedra!"

"What?"

"Take a breath."

"Oh. All right." She even sounded breathless. "If I must. If you'll—"

"Deedra."

"Okay. Just answer me."

"I'll try." Shannon chuckled. Once Deedra got on a roll, there was almost no stopping her. The woman could talk a mile a minute. "Nick is now cooperating with the interview, but I'm taking it slowly so as not to spook him. He's real touchy about all of it. I haven't called because I've been busy, and for that I apologize."

"Your mother calls me every day asking if I've heard from you."

"Really?" That surprised her. "Why didn't she call me?"

"She didn't want you to think she was—"

"Checking up on me," Shannon finished with her. It was one of her mother's favorite platitudes. *I don't want you to think I'm checking up on you, as if you're not your own person now, an independent adult. I don't want to make a nag of myself.*

Shannon and her mother were as different as night and day when it came to independence and self-confidence. Her mother claimed that both things must have skipped a generation, at least on the female side, because Shannon got more than her fair share, while her mother admittedly had little to none.

Shannon and Deedra both chuckled.

"If you're taking it slow," Deedra said, "then why are you so busy?"

"Oh, uh…" She and Deedra didn't generally have secrets from each other. They usually told each other everything. But this felt different. She wasn't ready to talk to anyone yet about her relationship—one-week fling?—with Nick. "Research, local color, that sort of thing."

"What kind of local color? You're in Texas. What are you doing, riding bulls?"

Shannon hooted. "No way, and you know it. There are some things that even I wouldn't do. However, it happens to be homecoming week here. I've been to a parade, a bonfire, a barbecue place, the nursing home—"

"Nurs—"

"Don't ask. It's complicated. I'll tell you all about it—" mostly "—when I get home. Tonight I'm going to help chaperone the homecoming dance."

"Get out. You are not."

"I am. My date is the high school's head custodian."

"Let me get this straight. You're going to a high-school dance."

"That's right."

"With the janitor."

"I am."

"Ahem. Might one ask, *pourquoi?*"

"Inquiring minds want to know?"

"They do," Deedra affirmed.

"It's more research."

"Don't tell me the janitor is the one you're interviewing."

"Okay, I won't tell you. What's wrong with janitors? Don't tell me you're a snob."

"Of course not. I just meant…I mean—"

"Yeah. That's what I caught myself thinking, too, when I got here. I was being a snob, myself. Janitor is an old and noble profession, just like any other."

"Who are you trying to convince? Me, or you?" Deedra needled.

"You. I'm already convinced. And, Dee?"

"Uh-oh. I know that tone. That's your serious tone, and I don't want to hear it when we're talking about high-school janitors and homecoming dances."

"Hear it anyway. You said he wasn't worth the trouble."

"I did."

"You were wrong," Shannon told her quietly.

Shannon was still smiling over Deedra's stunned silence followed by another endless stream of questions and demands about Nick, about her, about Nick and her, when the man in question knocked on her door.

"Oh, my," she said when she got a good look at him. The man cleaned up real nice, as her dad would have said. His dark gray suit accented the width of his shoulders, the length of his legs. The crisp white shirt contrasted beautifully with his dark olive complexion, and the tie added the perfect touch of panache. "You look fabulous."

Nick goggled. "You took the words right out of my mouth." Except, he thought, *fabulous* was way too poor a word for the vision of her. Her dress was plain, unadorned, unruffled black, long sleeved, high necked, ending just above her beautiful knees, and hugged every curve of her shapely body. Black three-inch heels made her legs look a mile and a half long.

He knew he was staring, he just couldn't seem to help himself. Didn't want to. "You've got legs."

Shannon snickered. "I've had them for quite a while. You've got a flower."

"What? Oh." Heat stung his cheeks. But

hell, if a guy couldn't make a fool out of himself over a pretty woman, then what good was he? It was homecoming, after all. He held out the clichéd pink carnation that Aunt Bev had forced him to buy. "This is for you."

The sheer delight on Shannon's face surprised him. Warmed him. Made him feel stupid and guilty for not thinking of giving her flowers on his own, and days ago. What was wrong with the men in her life that a simple corsage should surprise her so much?

"It's got elastic," he offered, "for your wrist, if you don't want to pin it to your dress." He wished he'd thought to wipe his palms before knocking on her door. Sweaty palms were hell on the male ego.

"Nick, you got me a corsage." Shannon's throat ached. Her eyes threatened to water. The last time a man had presented her with any type of flower had been when she'd graduated from college. The big, colorful bouquet had come from her father. She leaned forward and kissed him. "Thank you."

"No." He pulled her back for another kiss. "Thank you."

When he released her, she danced her way to the mirror and decided to pin the corsage to her dress. She made Nick help her, and it was a unique experience for them both. She ended up with one pinprick, while he jabbed himself three times.

Shannon kissed his injured finger, then grinned. "Do they give Purple Hearts for dating injuries?"

Everyone should be allowed to attend a high-school dance as an adult. Without the added angst of being a teenager, with all the cliques to navigate, the pimples to worry about, things looked entirely different.

With a final beat from the drums, the band ended the song. Nick wasted no time taking Shannon's hand and pulling her off the floor.

"I get to pick the next one we dance to," he told her.

"You don't like oldies rock?" Shannon teased. He might complain, but he'd been having a good time bopping around on the dance floor with her.

"I'm getting to old for those fast ones. I need air." He led her toward the door and the fresh air beyond.

Outside, the air was cool, the breeze strong and damp. She inhaled deeply. "Ah, that's good." She leaned against Nick's shoulder so no one could overhear. "Is your hip bothering you?"

He tensed. "No more than usual."

"Do you want to sit down for a while, or go for a walk?"

He drew to a halt and turned to face her. "Don't."

"Don't what?" She looked at him, trying to judge his reaction. She hadn't meant to mother him, but she couldn't seem to help it. But the lighting along the outside of the gym, while more than adequate, was garish and on the green side and did not help her read his mood.

"Don't worry about me." He took her hands in his. "Don't fuss over me."

"I only—"

"I know you don't mean to," he said with a smile tinged with sadness, "but when you bring it up, you make me feel like a cripple who needs to be taken care of."

For one brief instant, Shannon felt the blood start to drain from her face. "Nick—" Guilt settled like sickness in the pit of her stomach. She'd made him feel like a cripple? "You know I didn't mean it that way."

"I know." He rested his forehead against hers.

"I wouldn't ask about it if I didn't care."

"I know."

"You have to let people care about you, Nick."

He raised his head and looked up at the stars. "Why can't everybody just forget about my hip and leg? Why does it have to matter?"

Shannon pulled back to see him better. "You talk like you're ashamed of it." She felt a stirring of anger, both toward him and on his behalf. "Like it's somehow your fault that you were injured."

"I do not."

"You do. Oh, yes, you do," she repeated when he started to deny it. "That's why—"

"Why, what?"

At least he was as pissed off now as she was, Shannon thought. "We'll save this discussion for later. We've got an audience."

Nick jerked back as if he'd been shot. He looked around and, sure enough, at least a dozen students stood within earshot of them, several of them staring blatantly.

Nick was furious. Not at them, or Shannon, but at himself. He, who prized his privacy above nearly everything, had let himself be pulled into a deeply personal conversation in front of a bunch of teenagers.

"You're right." He forced a slow, deep breath. "We'll save it. I'm sorry I brought it up at all."

"You didn't," she said quietly. "I did, and

I'm sorry you took it wrong. If you recall, last night you were making jokes about the very same subject. But let me bring it up, and oh, no, can't do that."

"You weren't joking," he said tersely. "That was pity."

"I beg to differ. It was caring, concern. It was not pity." She glanced around again at all the eager ears and wanted to stomp her foot in frustration. "Come on. Let's go back in. I'm thirsty."

He took her by the hand and gave it a small squeeze. "Shannon?"

Finally she looked up at him. "Yes?"

"Can we rewind, here? You're right, I over-reacted. I feel like I've just punched a hole in something that wasn't meant to have a hole in it."

She stared up at him for a long moment,

the lights from the parking lot and the front of the gym casting her face in a garish light. Then suddenly she burst out in laughter. "Something that wasn't meant to have a hole in it? You are definitely not the writer of this duo."

Relief eased the tightness in his gut. They were back on an even keel. He gave her a mock glare. "You're making fun of me."

"Definitely. And I plan to do it again, real soon. Come inside and buy me a drink."

"Would you like a can, or a can?"

"Hmm, I believe I prefer a can. That's a dirty trick the organizers played, having tubs of canned soft drinks on ice and no punch bowl."

"Yeah," he agreed, "but it's harder to spike each individual soda can than it is a big bowl of punch."

The band started up with a slow ballad,

and Nick led her to the edge of the dance floor, where the crowd was thinnest, the lighting dimmest. "This," he whispered against her ear, "is my kind of dance."

Shannon felt the length of him pressed against her, hard and warm and right where she wanted to be. Had she been angry only minutes ago? Never mind that now. Now, he was holding her. Now they were swaying to the music. If now was all they had, she would live in the moment and be glad for it.

With her head resting against his chest, she felt a deep vibration and realized he was humming along with the song. Shannon smiled and fell a little bit more in love with him.

Chapter Ten

The dance officially ended at midnight, but it took another hour for everyone to clear out. Shannon was content to sit back and watch Nick maneuver the stragglers out the door as quickly as possible without offending any of them. He was good at it. Very good. The kids respected him, that much was plain. But they also liked him.

What did it say about a man, she wondered, that kids liked him, contemporaries sought his advice, women—at least this woman—found him irresistibly attractive, and his true calling was walking into burning buildings?

To her, it said one thing: Hero.

For now, she would keep that thought to herself.

The man in question came strolling back to her, his limp barely noticeable, even after all the dancing. But she wouldn't mention it. Not until she got him alone. And when she got him alone, she didn't want to talk. She wanted to hold him close and never let go.

The look on her face nearly took Nick's breath away. She wanted him. *Him,* Nick Carlucci. And she cared. Maybe more than cared, if she was feeling the things he felt, and from the way she looked at him, he would guess she did.

Yet she would leave him soon, unless one of them broke down and asked the other to cross the country. He wouldn't do that, not to either of them. He wouldn't go back to New York, not if he couldn't do the thing he was meant to do—fight fires. The city would be a constant reminder of how much of himself he had lost. He wouldn't last three months before he'd be unfit to live with.

And he wouldn't ask her to move here. Her life was in New York. Her job. No journalist gives up a job at the *New York Times* if writing for them is what they want to do. And Shannon did want that. If she gave that up for him and moved to Podunk, Texas, she would end up hating him.

They had this night, and tomorrow, at least.

Until she finished the interview. They couldn't keep postponing it. She couldn't stay away from her job forever.

He walked beside her to his car, leaving the English teacher, who was in charge of the dance, to lock up for the night. At the car, he opened the passenger door for Shannon, then got in and started the engine.

"I would like to be able to take you home with me."

Shannon laughed. "Wouldn't your aunt love that?"

"It would be awkward, you know? It's her house."

"You don't have to explain, Nick. No way do I want to get up in the middle of the night and run into her in the bathroom. We would both have a heart attack on the spot. I don't mind going to my place."

"Your place. You deserve better."

"Better than the Tribute Inn?" She smiled. "I've stayed in better. I've stayed in worse. Much worse. The only thing missing from this place is room service."

"You know I don't mean the room."

"You better not mean you."

Nick did not answer, and she did not pursue the subject. It seemed taboo and huge, and it sat there between them as Nick drove the short distance to the motel.

How foolish of him to bring up the subject in the first place. One of Shannon's most attractive qualities—and there were many— was her intelligence. She knew the score. She was away from home, having a fling with a man she would never have to see again. Good for a few laughs, a little sex—okay, a lot of really hot, steamy sex—but not much else.

She was going places with her life, while he…he'd already been to all the good places that had been there for him. This damn leg of his was never going to let him do what he was meant to do. It would always hold him back. Shannon deserved better than that.

Nick had known these things and come to accept them years ago. Funny, though, how they all faded away when he held out his hand for Shannon, to help her from the car. When he was touching her, he felt whole. Invincible.

"Are you going to tell me what you meant?" she asked as they climbed the stairs to her room where the two wings of the building met.

"No." He stopped at her door and stood aside while she unlocked it.

Once they were in, with the dead bolt latched, the lights on low, she turned to him.

"I'd like to challenge you about that, about my deserving better, but I doubt anything I say would change your mind."

He pulled her close and rested his cheek on the top of her head. "You always think I'm more than I am."

"And you think you're less. When you keep pushing people away, Nick, they eventually get the message."

He tightened his hold on her, pulling her deeper into his embrace. "I'm not pushing you away. I'm not. But you'll go anyway, no matter what, so why don't we leave it alone for now?"

She flexed her hands across his back. "Sounds like a plan."

Nick turned his head, just as she turned hers, and their lips met. Tonight there was no sudden eruption of passion. This was a slow, poignant simmer, one to savor with lingering touches, long glances, hearts beating together. It was slow and gentle, and they climbed the slope and reached the peak together.

Neither spoke. Nick didn't know what to say. He'd never experienced anything so moving in his life. She touched something deep down in his soul, and it was both frightening and soothing, even as it aroused.

Shannon couldn't speak. Her throat was too tight with unshed tears. She had to keep her eyes closed so he wouldn't see, but she feared they would leak any minute. She knew goodbye when she felt it. That's what this had been. The most bittersweet goodbye. Her heart was shattered.

But she couldn't give up without at least a token effort, could she? She took a deep breath and dove off the cliff. "Come home with me, Nick."

For a long time, Nick didn't move, didn't say anything. He was afraid even to breathe. Those words, those precious words, sang softly in his blood. *Come home with me.*

She made it sound so easy. Pack a bag, walk out the door, get on a plane. *Come home with me.*

Slowly he turned, with her still in his arms, until they lay on their sides facing each other. "I have never," he said softly, his heart swelling in his throat, "been so flattered, so blessed to have you ask me that. I am humbled, Shannon. And stunned."

"Why stunned? You have to know I've fallen in love with you."

"You have to know you're not alone there, right? I've fallen just as far for you."

She trailed her fingers lightly over his cheek. "Well, then? Shouldn't we do something about that?"

"I can't go back to New York."

"Will you tell me why?"

He pulled back and eyed her critically. "Are you going to put this in your book?"

"Not if you don't want me to."

He thought about it a minute, then gave a single nod. "It's hard to admit. Where I come from a guy does not talk about his feelings. A real man doesn't have feelings."

Shannon nodded sadly. "I know exactly what you mean. I'm just luckier, because girls are expected to have feelings and it's perfectly acceptable to let them out whenever and wherever. Usually."

"Not us. We were big, macho men. Firefighters, all three of us. It wasn't just what we did, it was who we were. We *were* the job. Like you. You're not a writer only when you're actually writing, or sitting at your desk. You *are* a writer, no matter where you are. It's the same with me. I'm a firefighter, but it goes deeper than that. I couldn't live in New York and not do what I was born to do."

"Maybe if you—"

"I tried, Shannon. I tried for two years, and it nearly killed me. I started drinking to numb the ache inside that wouldn't let up. I drank for most of those two years. I was a mess. A pathetic mess. When I finally crawled out of the bottle and cleaned myself up, I knew the only way I could live was if I left the city."

"There are jobs that don't—"

"Desk jobs. That might be fine for some, but not for me. Talk about your reminders of what you can't do anymore, surround yourself with able-bodied firefighters."

Shannon rolled onto her back and threw her arm across her eyes. "It sounds like you've given this a lot of thought."

"Every minute of every day."

She rolled back to her side and stroked his face again. "I am so, so sorry, Nick. Sorry you've lost such a big part of yourself. I'm sorry you don't want to go back. If I could do or say anything to make it easier for you, to take away your pain, I would. That's not pity," she added, placing her fingers over his lips to keep him from speaking. "It's love. I love you."

The words crashed into Nick like a wave, inundating every cell, every nerve, lifting him higher than he'd ever been. They stole his breath. They stopped his heart, then sent it racing. She loved him. Shannon Malloy loved him.

He looked her in the eyes and spoke. "I have never been given such a treasured gift in all my life. I love you, too, Shannon. It doesn't change the fact that you have to go home, and I have to stay here, but I love you."

Elation and sorrow fought for supremacy in Shannon's heart, making it hard to breathe. She inched away from Nick, hoping for more air. "You give me hope then snatch it away in the same sentence. Is that what love is to you?"

Nick's eyes closed. "No. To me, love is about caring and honesty and respect. It's about wanting what's best for someone else, over and above what you might want for yourself."

Shannon sniffed. Her eyes were about to leak. She sat up and hugged her knees, her back toward Nick. "Is that what you're doing? Deciding what's best for me?"

"No, that's just a side benefit of knowing what I am and am not capable of."

She hung her head and swallowed twice. Once for her tears, the other, her pride. "I notice you aren't asking me to stay here."

Nick couldn't stand to see her huddled there, alone and hurting. Because of him. He sat up and took her in his arms. "I would ask in an instant—I would beg—if I thought we had a chance in hell of making it work between us."

Silence was his answer.

"You know I'm right, don't you?"

She sniffed again.

"You're just getting your career in gear. You'd have to leave the *Times*. Your newspaper career would be reduced to a weekly gossip column in the *Tribute Banner.* You'd eventually blame me for your career going south, and even if you didn't, I'd blame myself. Then we'd both be miserable."

She gave him a crooked smile. "That's because you blame yourself for everything."

Look at her, he thought in awe. He had just kicked her in the teeth and she was cracking a joke. Sort of. "I guess I do. Right now we're both pretty miserable. That's my fault."

"Oh, pul-eeze." She rolled her eyes. "Get over yourself, Carlucci."

"I guess that love thing comes and goes, huh?"

She gave a decidedly unladylike snort of laughter. "You're the one who said love was about honesty. I just calls 'em as I sees 'em."

"Wanna argue about it?"

Her smile softened. "What I'd rather do is finish our interview."

Finish, so she could leave him once and for all. But how could he tell her no? He could put it off a little while, but it wasn't going away. He would just have to do as she'd suggested and get over himself.

"All right," he agreed. "But I'm not being tape recorded without my pants on." He scooted to the edge of the bed and reached for his slacks.

She snickered and crawled out of the bed. "It's an audiotape, not video."

"I don't care. I'm not doing this naked."

In furtherance of separating business from pleasure, she decided to make the symbolic gesture of conducting the interview at the small table instead of on the bed. She set up her recorder, got out her pad and a couple of pens, along with her laptop, and asked Nick to take the chair opposite her.

After stating the date and time for the tape, she asked Nick if he would mind telling her again, with the tape running, what he'd told her earlier about why he'd left New York.

He agreed, but she had to practically pull the information out of him one word at a time.

"You don't want this sob story in there," he protested.

"This is exactly the type of information I want in here," she argued. "It's this information that might help lead to better counseling options for first responders across the board."

Nick eyed her carefully. "So that's what this is all about."

"In part, yes. If you'll talk about your experiences with the media, it might enlighten a few of them, too."

"An enlightened media? You'll pardon me, but I think that's an oxymoron."

"Shame," she said with a mock frown.

And so Nick hashed it all out again, this time for the tape. All his rotten experiences since waking up in the hospital and being told he would never walk again. Being told he was a hero.

She took him through it all, the hospital, the therapy, the euphoria over getting his legs back, the devastation in learning he couldn't do the job anymore. The refusal to believe it. The grief for the department, his father and brother, the loss of his career. The drinking and the blur of months that passed in an alcoholic haze.

Nick gave her everything she asked, up to and including his satisfaction in pushing a broom all day.

"You really like it?" she asked.

"I do. I mean, I'd rather be with FDNY, but this will do."

"Custodian. Janitor. You know some people look down on a job like that," she stated.

"Some snobs, maybe. Even I did at first, but it's a big job with an incredible responsibility, being in charge of the entire physical aspect of the school, from maintenance to appearance to security. I'm even in charge of jump-starting cars with dead batteries," he added with a grin.

"You're kidding."

"Nope, it's official. The principal even announced it at the assembly at the beginning of the term. If you have car trouble, Mr. Nick will help you get going."

She cocked her head. "Do you see yourself as a loser?"

He paused. "Not a loser. More of a has-been," he said candidly.

"Can you explain the difference to me?"

"In my past, I *have been* exactly what I believe I was born to be. A New York City firefighter. I've lost that now." His voice quieted. "But that doesn't make me a loser, because a certain woman I know says she loves me, and she's a really smart lady. She wouldn't fall for a loser."

Shannon's eyes stung. She studied her notes. When she felt more composed, she looked at him again. "Okay, we've talked about everything in your life since 9/11, except the day itself. Are you willing to take me through that day with you?"

Nick exhaled sharply. Here it was, then. He was either going to talk, or call himself a coward for the rest of his life. Those other men she had interviewed had spoken openly. Nick could do no less. But first he had to let the ache in his throat die down.

"Okay." He took another deep breath, then turned sideways in his chair so that he wasn't facing her directly. He couldn't look directly at her and say the things he needed to say. "Okay. It was my day off, but Dad and Vinnie were on. I was sleeping in. The woman next door, Mrs. Bonetti, came banging on the door, telling me to look at the smoke and turn on the TV. I couldn't believe what I was seeing—it was like something out of a movie. It couldn't be real. But it was."

He told her about worrying about his dad and brother. About racing to get to the station house in time to learn of the first building's collapse. Panic had seized him. The station was empty but for the two probies who had signed on the week before. It was their day off, too. They'd come in and not known what to do. Nick ordered them into their turnout gear. Screw the phones. Every man would be needed down there.

All he was able to think was the buildings, the buildings fell. Disaster. *Dad. Vinnie.*

Everyone was in a daze, trying to orient themselves.

"And somehow, when the cloud dissipated enough so that you could see where you were going, I found myself on top of this huge pile of rubble. I mean, huge. The dust that settled out of the air piled up so deep, I sank to my ankles in the damn stuff. I still have nightmares about that dust now and then."

"I remember the dust," Shannon murmured.

"And it was so quiet—it was weird. It was

like funeral-home quiet, except for the pass alarms. Hundreds of them." He took a deep breath. "I told myself that if we could dig to just the right spot, we'd find a pocket, and people.

"But we didn't. Are you sure you want to hear this?" he asked her.

Shannon gave him a tired smile. "I've heard it all a dozen times, and I was there myself later that day. Don't pretty it up for me, just tell it as you experienced it."

Nick took another deep breath. This talking business wasn't too bad. He figured he was doing okay. He told her in frank terms about the nightmarish search.

Nobody knew where his dad and Vinnie were, but their company had been there since right after the first plane hit. Nick knew his guys, he knew his father and brother. They would have been inside the building, climbing the stairs to get to the people trapped by the fire.

"I was frantic, wanting to find someone. We all were. Then, by some miracle, sometime that afternoon I stepped on a piece of concrete that shifted, and I thought I heard something. I couldn't see anything, but I started shifting this piece and that one, and found a man."

"Oh," Shannon breathed. "Oh, Nick."

"Wait." Nick shook his head. "I got him out and I could tell he'd been crushed pretty badly. I could tell by his uniform he was a Port Authority officer. His badge had been torn off, along with half his shirt."

Shannon sucked in a sharp breath.

"Shannon?"

She shook her head. "Sorry. Go on."

"I'm sorry." He took her hand. "Your dad was a Port Authority cop, wasn't he? I shouldn't be telling you this."

"Yes, you should. Go on. Please."

"All right, if you're sure."

"I'm sure."

He studied her face for a moment. She met his gaze squarely and seemed to be fine. "Okay. I tried to give him my mask so he could breath something besides dust, but he waved it away. I've always regretted not knowing his name. He died in my arms."

"Oh, Nick, that must have been devastating."

"Even worse," he told her. "Because I never knew his name, I never got to tell his family that right before he died, he said to tell his girls that he died with the sun on his face. He made me promise. It seemed important that they know. Shannon?"

Shannon stared at Nick in shock. Chills raced up and down her spine. Her hands shook so hard, she couldn't hold her pen. It clattered onto the table.

"Shannon, what's wrong?"

"Describe him."

"Who, the cop?"

Her ears were buzzing. She shook her head to make them stop. She did not want to miss a word of this. "*What did he look like?* Tall? Short? Dark hair? Light? Bald? What did he look like?"

"He was tall, a little overweight. Thick dark hair. At least I think it was dark underneath all that dust and ash."

Shannon's heart beat faster with every word.

"He had a tattoo. I just remembered that."

She straightened away from the back of her chair and stared at him so hard it was a wonder the air between them didn't crack. "What kind of tattoo?"

"A rose. No, a shamrock. I remember now. With the word *blarney* beneath it."

A sharp cry escaped her throat. She reached across the table and clamped on to Nick's hand, squeezing so tight she was probably bruising herself. "Nick—you found my father."

Chapter Eleven

In a heartbeat, Shannon was around the tiny table and in Nick's lap. They held on to each other like the last two people to make it onto the life raft before the ship sank. And they cried.

Never in a million years would Nick have thought to find himself weeping in a woman's arms. It wasn't manly. It wasn't macho Italiano, as his father would have said. Only a sissy would cry.

Well, this sissy cried his eyes out—after all, he'd been holding it in for five years—and in the process, he felt a new lightening inside himself.

Now that his tears were dried, he noticed that Shannon was quieting in his arms. He stood and carried her to the bed and lay down beside her.

"You will never know," she said, her voice unsteady, "what this means to me. What it will mean to my mother after all these years." With her arms around his neck, she squeezed him tight.

"His face still haunts my dreams." He was rambling, but couldn't seem to help it. "I wanted more than anything to be able to find someone, to help someone. When I finally found him, I was too late. Too damn late."

She pushed him away and sat up, glaring at him. "That's nothing to do with you," she said fiercely. "If he died that fast, then it had been too late the minute it happened. Is *this* what's been eating at you all these years? That you didn't save my father?"

"You don't understand."

"I think I do. Get this straight, Nick. You are not responsible for my father's death."

"I told you, in my head, I know I'm not responsible. But my head's got no control over the guilt I feel, or the uselessness."

"How can that be? How can you feel useless when you *did* save people? You saved seven men, specifically, one of whom is your current fire chief's cousin. Or is that part of the problem? When you finally are able to save someone, it nearly kills you, and robs you of the way of life you loved. It would be perfectly natural for you to resent saving those men."

"I don't resent them. Good God, no," he cried, sitting up. "It never even occurred to me to wish I hadn't done what I did. Maybe it should have. Maybe that kind of resentment would have been easier to live with than feeling useless. Or, maybe then I would have been resentful and useless."

"Maybe you just like carrying the weight of the world on your shoulders."

"Not anymore," he claimed. "I can't get farther than a couple of steps carrying any weight at all these days. Which takes me right back to Tribute, Texas."

"It could take you right back to the FDNY if you'd let it."

"We've already had that discussion."

"With your background there are a number of jobs you could do. You could be an instructor, dispatcher, administrator."

He shook his head no while she rattle on. He'd thought of those things himself, but a desk job? It would kill him.

"You could go into arson investigation," she added.

"I'm not qualified."

"Then get qualified. Unless you truly love the position of high-school custodian, do *something* besides hide out here in Tribute. That's what you're doing, you know."

"Shannon—"

"What about your father, your brother?" she cried. "Do you think they'd be pleased to see you shut yourself off from the life you loved? And what about us?"

"We had the *us* discussion. There is no us. What we've had is something I'll always remember, and it's been terrific, but when you leave for New York, it ends."

Shannon reeled. He might as well have slapped her in the face. Earlier he'd said he wouldn't go to New York and wouldn't ask her to stay here with him. But he hadn't said it was over. Hadn't said they were through. Now he wasn't just closing the door on them, he was slamming it shut.

Her eyes were barely dry from her previous crying jag, and now they filled again. "No," she said, fighting the tears down while she rose from the bed. "It ends now. Right now."

"Shannon, I—"

"Don't, Nick." She forced herself to look him in the eye. "It's better this way, don't you think? A clean break?"

"You call this clean? Look, I'm sorry, Shannon. I've hurt you, and that was never my intention." A few minutes later, when he had put on his shoes, gathered his wallet and keys, he headed toward the door.

Shannon held her breath, hoping her control would last long enough. She was doing fine. She was going to make it.

Then he stopped. Right in front of her, he stopped, turned, and placed a soft, heart-breaking kiss on her cheek. A tear trickled down, and he sipped it from her skin. "Don't cry because of me. I'm not worth it." He walked to the door, then paused again. "Have a nice life, Shannon Malloy. You are one special lady."

When the door closed behind him, she carefully lowered herself to the bed, where she quietly cried herself to sleep.

* * *

The only way Nick was going to sleep that night was if someone whacked him over the head with something hard and heavy. That was his determination when he looked at his bedside clock again for the third time in twenty minutes. It still wasn't dawn. It wasn't even 4:00 a.m. yet.

He might have been able to nod off but for seeing the tears in Shannon's eyes every time he closed his own.

She just didn't understand what it meant to him to be able to *do* something. To make a difference.

Yeah, okay, he could pep talk himself until he was blue in the face about the importance of a good school custodian in the lives of the students, but it wasn't the FDNY. It wasn't the life he'd grown up reaching for, knowing it was his for the taking.

To hell with this. He threw the covers aside and got out of bed. It was time to walk off the ache in his hip. A little fresh air might also help him sleep. It was Sunday. He didn't need to be anywhere. He could sleep as late as he wanted.

Except he didn't want to sleep late. He wanted to see Shannon tomorrow. He shouldn't. He should simply let her go. She would go, in any case, so why complicate it any more than it already was?

But at least he could sit in the café and watch for her rental car to drive by on its way out of town. That way he would at least know when his heart was completely out of reach.

He grabbed an old pair of jeans that didn't smell too bad from the floor of his closet, put on socks and walking shoes, and a sweatshirt. It had been dipping down toward forty degrees when he'd come home.

He tiptoed through the house so as not to wake Bev, then struck out through his neighborhood, setting every dog in the area to barking. Can't pull anything over on these guys. Now, if he'd been a burglar, they wouldn't have made a sound, he was sure.

As much as he loved New York, Nick had come to love this small Texas town, and he'd come to love the quiet peacefulness of night. He would like it even better, he thought, if it weren't for the faint whiff of smoke on the breeze. The remains of the bonfire were still in the air.

At the end of his neighborhood he turned toward Main, intending to cross and amble over toward the school. Might as well do a walk-by while he was out.

Sure enough, the smell of smoke grew stronger the closer he got to the school and the field behind it where the giant pile of dried brush had met its fiery end.

But wait a minute. He was still too far away for the smell to be so strong. That fire had been nothing but cold ashes since Thursday night, and this was Sunday morning.

Maybe some kids had decided to revive the fire after the dance. Great, just what they needed. Teenagers, fire and, most certainly, alcohol. Never a good mix, no matter how you looked at it.

As he crossed Main, something in his gut tightened. He stopped and stood there, in the middle of the street, waiting. He didn't know what the question was, but an answer was trying to form. Something was wrong. The smoke was wrong. The wind had shifted and was coming out of the north tonight. If the bonfire had been relit with thirty-foot flames, he wouldn't be able to smell it from here because the wind would carry the smoke and odor south. What he smelled was from right there in town. To his right. Toward—

"Sweet heaven." Smoke was boiling from the vicinity of the Tribute Inn. "Shannon."

He started jogging as fast as he could, but he didn't want to risk his leg going out from under him until he knew Shannon was all right. Dammit, he was going to have to start carrying his cell phone on these middle-of-the-night walks. But in all the time he'd lived there, he'd had no need for it.

He pushed himself faster, his heart starting to pound. Not from exertion, but from fear. The closer he got to the motel, the more pronounced his limp, and the more certain he became that the motel was on fire. When he passed the grocery store, the motel came into view. He couldn't see flames, but there was smoke. Lots of smoke.

Where was a phone? He had to call 911.

As he thought it, he heard the alarm go off at the fire station. He was amazed that he heard anything over the roaring in his ears, much less an alarm from half a mile away. But he was positive that was what he heard. A firefighter knew the sound.

He didn't know how long it would take them to get here. He knew that no one slept over at the station. They were all volunteers and were seldom needed. They all had pagers. When a call came in to 911, those whose names were on the duty roster for that time were automatically paged.

He couldn't wait. When he reached the

motel, flames shot out of the second-floor roof way too close to Shannon's room for comfort. It looked as if it may have started in the office, at the far end of that wing. He ran up to the first door and banged on it, shouting, "Fire! Everybody out! The motel is on fire!"

He didn't know how many rooms were occupied, but there were seven cars in the parking lot. All the rooms were dark at this time of night. No way to tell which were occupied, which weren't. So he limped down the row of first-floor rooms as fast as he could, pounding on each door and shouting.

When he reached the fourth door, someone came out from the first door he'd pounded on.

"Oh, my God," the man cried.

"Get everybody out. Pound on the doors, yell, wake them up. I'll get the upstairs."

Nick didn't wait to see if the man followed through.

He pounded on one door after another, then stopped cold in his tracks. A wall of fire blocked him from reaching Shannon's room.

The fire was noisy now, all furious roaring, crashing, popping, exploding. All around him people screamed and yelled and cried. And from down the street came the beautiful roar of the fire engine. Praise God.

But he couldn't wait. Shannon was in there.

Just as the fire engine pulled up, Nick leaped through the wall of flames. For one heart-stopping instant, he was engulfed. No air, only searing heat and flame.

Then, poof, he was out the other side. He made it to Shannon's door without anything important getting burned off, but his leg was screaming at him.

He pounded on Shannon's door and yelled her name. "Fire! Shannon, fire!"

He got no response. The smoke was thick here, the flames getting closer. They completely blocked his view of the parking lot. No help from that area yet. He pounded harder, wishing frantically that he knew how to pick a lock.

The surface of the door wasn't hotter than it should be, so that was something. There was no fire on the other side.

He threw himself at the door, to no avail. With his weight on his good leg, he kicked out with his bad one but couldn't get any real force behind it. The jogging had taken its toll. If he switched legs and stood on his bad one, he feared he'd fall. The bad one wouldn't support him. He didn't mind falling, but if he couldn't get up and move, he couldn't help Shannon. He was going to have to break the window beside the door.

After three awkward tries, he ended up using his elbow, somewhat protected by the sleeve of his sweatshirt.

He didn't have the time or the patience to make sure every shard was out of his way. He climbed through, tearing flesh and fabric as he went.

He needn't have worried about letting in smoke. The room was filled with it.

"Shannon!"

She was on the bed, curled up in a tight ball, unconscious. Nick's heart stopped. He called her name again and felt for a pulse. He couldn't tell if he found one or not; his had started up again and was hammering too hard.

Then, suddenly, she coughed.

"Shannon, baby, come on now, we have to

go. There's a fire and we have to get out, but you have to get up and walk."

She coughed so hard she passed out again.

The situation, as Nick saw it, was dangerous, bordering on grim. He couldn't carry her out. His leg wasn't taking any weight at all now, after the jogging and the kicking. If he carried her to the door it would be a miracle, and after that were the flames. If she didn't come to, they were screwed.

The crew would get the fire knocked down, but he had no desire simply to hope they got to this back room in time. As far as he knew, no one was aware that he and Shannon were there.

The smoke was getting thicker, choking him, stinging his eyes. He pulled her down to the floor and fumbled for the bedside phone. No dial tone. The fire must have already burned through the lines.

Cell. She had a cell phone. Where was it? Had she put it back in her purse? Where was the purse? Where the hell was the damn purse?

"Shannon! Wake up. Come on, wake up."

No response.

Nick swore again and finally found her purse, but the phone wasn't in it. The table. Maybe she'd left it…*there*. He had it.

He called 911, wondering if he would get the local service or something else.

It was the county 911 dispatcher, thank God. He told her their situation and asked that someone contact the fire chief at the scene and have him direct his spray toward the back corner. The woman tried to keep him on the phone, but he had to make preparations in case the fire decided to come in through that broken window before the crew could knock it down. He would have to make a stand in the bathroom.

He tried to carry Shannon that far, but she was too limp and his leg was too weak. He ended up half dragging her to the tub, thanking God for slow renovations. The tub was an old cast-iron job that, if nothing else, wouldn't melt and fuse with their skin. Of course, there was every possibility that they could end up beyond caring, but not as long as Nick had so much as one breath left in his body.

He left Shannon on the floor next to the tub, then crawled back and pulled the sheets and blanket from the bed. They would make good wet wraps and help filter the air for breathing. He was about to close the bathroom door and seal them in with a wet towel along the bottom to help keep any more smoke from getting in when he re-membered her computer. If they lived through this and she realized he had let her computer burn, she would kill him.

He made one last foray through the room, grabbing only what he thought she would consider essential. Purse, cell phone, notepad, computer. Shoes beside the bed. He stuffed the cell phone in her purse, and everything else in the bag for her laptop. By then his bad leg was worse than useless, making crawling on all fours impossible, so he belly-crawled. There was more air at the floor level, anyway.

Any minute now, he kept thinking, the pipe would be trained on their door and the fire would retreat. Any minute.

But now the fire was at their door. He could hear it, feel the increased heat. In another couple of seconds—yes. There. The drapes on the broken window. He should have pulled them down, but now they were on fire. Time was running out.

He made it back into the bathroom and, in what was probably a useless gesture, considering the amount of smoke already there and the nearness of the fire, he closed them in and put a soaking wet towel over the crack beneath the door. Then he turned on the water in the tub and quickly soaked the bed linens. He got Shannon and her belongings into the tub, climbed in after them, and wrapped them all in sopping wet sheets with the blanket beneath them to protect them as much as possible in case the tub got hot.

"Shannon?" He was too out of breath to be able to find a pulse on her. He was too busy praying to slow his breathing. It was one thing to walk into a burning building and rescue strangers, while wearing full turnout gear, breathing air through a tank and knowing your brothers-in-arms, as it were, had your back. That was his calling. He had been good at it.

But to be on the other end, to be the one needing rescue, knowing he could not get Shannon out to safety, left a bitter taste in his mouth.

God, he could feel the tub getting hot. The flames must be licking at it from below because if the door was on fire he would hear the sound. He could raise the sheet and look, but he didn't. He held Shannon close in his arms, turning so that he practically lay on top of her to shield her as much as possible with his own body.

And he prayed. He had already done all he

could. He wasn't interested in letting Fate take him just yet. He prayed for a big, hard stream of water. He prayed for Lon to guide his men well. He prayed that the 911 operator got through to Lon.

Then he heard the roar of the fire. The door was burning. The wall, too, probably. Not good. Not good at all.

Suddenly—*boom!*

His heart jumped. Explosion? Fire? Water? What?

An instant later he heard a shout. He couldn't make out any words, but it was a voice.

They were coming.

The parking lot and three full blocks of Main Street were awash in people and vehicles and fire hoses. The fire was out now, but no one seemed anxious to leave.

Nick stood beside Shannon and held her hand, grateful to feel her squeeze his. The paramedics determined that she'd been rendered unconscious by smoke inhalation and had her on oxygen. When she'd started coughing earlier, it had seemed to Nick as if she might never stop. The paramedics would have insisted she go to the hospital and have a doctor look her over, but the doctor had come to them.

"You're going to be fine," Nick reminded her now. "The doctor will check you again in an hour, and then I can take you home."

Shannon felt as if she were emerging from a deep sleep. She guessed she was, essentially, since she'd been unconscious. But she was catching up fast. Fire. Smoke. Nick. Home?

She pulled off the oxygen mask so she

could talk easier. "How…you came. How did you know?" God, her throat ached.

He put the mask back on her and told her about being unable to sleep, about walking, smelling smoke.

"Thank God you did," she said with feeling.

"You're right about that, Ms. Malloy," Lon Wallace said, standing on the other side of her gurney. "If he hadn't got you into the tub and covered you with wet sheets, then called to let us know where you were, we wouldn't have gotten to you in time."

"Don't oversell it," Nick said with a crooked smile.

"I'm not. I guess you didn't notice the bed when you came out."

She pulled the mask away. "What about the bed?"

Nick put the mask back in place. They

tussled a moment and she resorted to merely lifting it away from her mouth to speak rather than pulling it all the way off her face.

Lon gave a nod of approval. "The bed is where he found you when he got here, right?"

"I was asleep."

Lon patted her arm. "I don't mean to scare you any more than you already are, but that bed is toast now."

Shannon's mouth went dry. "Toast?" she croaked.

Nick frowned at the chief. "We get the picture."

Lon winked at Shannon. "But then, we already knew he was a hero, didn't we?"

She looked from Lon to Nick, who looked away and stared at the skeletal remains of the motel. The entire end where her room had been was destroyed, including the office.

She would have been gone, too, were it not for Nick, but he didn't like hearing it and wouldn't want the credit. "Some of us did."

Nick had to figure that the only reason Shannon agreed to go home with him instead of checking into another motel was that she was too exhausted to make the effort. And maybe still too shaken to want to be alone.

They drove her car, which was only dinged slightly by the effort to put out the fire. Bev greeted them at the front door, pulling her nephew into her arms. It seemed that someone she knew had seen Nick at the fire and had heard about how he had rushed into a wall of flame and had called Bev to tell her about it.

"What can I do for you? Oh, you poor things, look at you. Do you want a shower first, or food? Or do you want to just go straight to bed? I've got a spare nightgown you're welcome to, and in the morning we can see about getting you some clothes."

A tear leaked from Shannon's eye, and it nearly killed Nick.

"Thank you," she croaked. "I would hug you, but you don't want me to touch you like this."

For the first time, Nick realized that the two of them were covered in black soot—as Bev was, thanks to his embrace—and they reeked of smoke.

"Don't you worry about that. Come into the kitchen for a minute, both of you." She poured them each a glass of orange juice with orders to drink every drop.

"Then you can shower. I'll go set out some things you might need," she said to Shannon. "If I miss anything, just let me know."

"Thank you, Bev. You're a godsend."

"You're more than welcome. Nick, my boy, I won't scold you for leaping through a wall of flames—"

Shannon shuddered at the words.

"—because you saved Shannon. Bless you both. Now, I'll get out of your way. The house is yours, dear," she said, patting Shannon's shoulder.

When she left them there in the kitchen, Shannon turned to Nick. "You saved my life, and you saved my work, my computer. You even saved my purse with my wallet, ID and cash. Am I allowed to say thank you?"

He ducked his head. "If you want, but it's not necessary."

"I want, and it is necessary. You weren't just doing your job, because it's not your job anymore. But you did it anyway." She kissed his sooty lips. "I'm alive right now because of you. Don't you *ever* call yourself a useless has-been again."

Shannon showered first, then Nick. She slept in his bed, curled up in his arms, and neither spoke.

Nick had gone for a walk because he couldn't sleep. Now here he was, back in bed, with sleep not even a remote possibility. He would not relinquish a single second of his time with Shannon by sleeping. She would leave him soon enough.

Maybe she felt the same desperation that was threatening to choke him because she turned to him and kissed his lips. Without a word, they kissed, they touched, they stroked. They made love so slowly, so sweetly, it almost didn't seem real.

When they slipped off the edge together, it was warm and sweet and gentle. And afterward, he fell asleep, forever grateful to feel her alive and safe in his arms one more time.

Chapter Twelve

When Nick woke the next morning, Shannon was gone.

No note, no message. Just…gone.

He knew without checking that she hadn't gone to another motel. She was on her way home. It was time; she had no more reason to stay.

He wanted to pull the covers over his head

and tell the world to go away, but he had promised to talk to Lon about the fire, let the man ask his questions.

He crawled out of bed, stepped into a pair of jeans that didn't smell like smoke, and followed the aroma of coffee to the kitchen.

Bev stood there, leaning against the counter, arms folded over her chest, waiting for him. She didn't look particularly welcoming. "So you let her go, did you?"

He grunted and headed for the nearest empty coffee mug so he could fill it. "Good morning to you, too."

"Go ahead, get yourself a cup. You look like you need it."

"Th—" His voice croaked. Damn smoke. He swallowed and tried again. "Thanks."

When he filled his mug and took a seat at the breakfast table, she joined him.

"Nick, I've never been one to pry, you know that."

"I sense a *but* coming."

"Nobody ever said you were stupid. Until now. And that's exactly what I'm saying. You are the *dumbest* creature on God's green earth to let that woman go home without you."

Nick hung his head and let her words batter him.

"Well? What do you have to say for yourself?"

Slowly he raised his head to look at her. "Not a thing. You'll get no argument out of me."

"So? Don't get me wrong, I love you and love sharing a home with you. But what are you doing here if she's on her way back to New York? Nick, talk to me. I don't understand this at all. You are so obviously in love with her, and she with you. You do know that, don't you?"

"I know that," he told her. "Love isn't our problem."

"If you love each other, then you can work anything out."

He was shaking his head before she finished speaking. "You know I can't live in New York anymore."

"You mean you chose not to."

"All right." Dammit, he didn't need this right now. "I chose not to spend every single day staring into the face of the thing I was born to do, and not be able to *do* it."

"That's nothing but sheer pride talking, Nick. If you want to be around fires, be an instructor, or a dispatcher. Become an arson investigator."

Those were the same things Shannon had

told him. The same things he'd told himself a long time ago. The same suggestions his commander had given him when Nick had left the hospital five years ago. He told Bev the same thing he'd told them. "It's not the same."

"No, it isn't. When did you get to be so special that you have to have everything exactly the way you want it?"

Nick felt a painful throbbing start behind his eyes. It had been a long, long time since he'd been scolded. At his age, it was a little hard to take, but he sat there and took it. It was starting to sink in that maybe, just maybe, he had it coming.

Shannon was beyond numb and approaching zombie status by the time she made it home. She hadn't had a reservation, so she'd had to sit around the Dallas-Fort Worth airport all day and catch the 6:30 p.m. flight to LaGuardia. By the time she landed, taxied, caught a cab and got into her apartment, it was past midnight.

Just think how late it might have been if she'd had any luggage to check. Any luggage at all. Thank you, mister fire, for incinerating my clothes.

Thank you, Nick, for saving my purse and laptop.

And that was the last time she was going to think about Nick. Except, of course, for however many days it took to write and edit his chapter in her book.

How was she going to keep her feelings out of the writing?

She was going to be the professional journalist she hoped she'd always been, that's how.

But first, she would sleep. Tomorrow she

had to report back to the paper. And call her mother and Deedra. And somehow, through it all, manage to act like a normal person who had not recently met, and lost, the love of her life.

Shannon managed to make it through that first horrible day, and then the next one and the next. She worked at the paper during the day and found a hundred different things to keep her busy each evening. Busy, as in, no time to work on that certain chapter in her manuscript.

There was no hurry, really. She had two more months until her deadline. In a few more days, maybe a couple of weeks, she would get her act together and get it finished.

Then another day went by, and one more after that.

Enough, she told herself. This was stupid, moping around as if her dog had just died. It wasn't a dog; it was only a man. *The* man, true, and with him was her heart, but what the heck. She didn't need it to give to anyone else in the foreseeable future. Nick was gone.

There. She had thought his name and the world did not come to an end. She marched to the closet where she had stashed her laptop when she'd come home from Texas and hauled it out.

Oh, God, the bag and all its contents reeked of smoke.

She spent most of the evening cleaning everything carefully, doing everything she could think of to get rid of the smell. When she went to work the next morning, she would leave everything from her bag—laptop, notepad, tape recorder—sitting out in her living room, ready for use when she came home.

Everything seemed to still be in working order. Even the tape in her recorder still played, although she wouldn't be listening to it anytime soon. Not the last part, she thought with a smile. It seemed that she had never turned it off that last night. She had inadvertently captured the sounds of their lovemaking.

It felt good to smile again. She was going to be all right. She *was* all right.

And then she went to bed and dreamed of Nick. The next morning, the ache of missing him was so strong she almost convinced herself to stay home and wallow in her misery.

But she did go to work. Whatever had brought on the good mood of the night before had deserted her, but with grim determination, she kept her misery to herself. She *would* be fine, dammit. She would be terrific.

No more putting off that chapter in her manuscript. That night when she got home, she changed into her sweats and settled down on the sofa, with all her writing materials spread out around her. And she sat there and stared.

It was one thing to say she was going to write about Nick, but it was another actually to do it. Writing about him would be like bringing him into her home with her. Wouldn't he then haunt her every day and night after that?

Someone knocked on her door. They must have played the *keep pressing buttons until someone lets you in* game because she hadn't buzzed anyone up. Frowning, she went to the door, double checked that the dead bolt was engaged, and looked through her peephole.

Nick. "Nick?" She fumbled the lock three times before getting it open. "Nick! Where did you come from? What are you doing here? Is everything all right?"

He stood in her doorway, his hands buried in the pockets of his brown bomber jacket, an expression on his face that she could not read.

"I came from Texas," he answered. "To see you. And no, everything's not all right."

Her heart skipped a beat. She grabbed his hand and pulled him through the door. She wanted to fling her arms around him and hold on until the next ice age and beyond. But he didn't look all that approachable, and she did have her pride, after all. She released his hand and turned to close and lock her door before facing him again. "What's wrong?" she asked.

"We didn't finish."

Shannon swallowed and eyed him warily, afraid to hope, unable to do otherwise. "Didn't finish what?"

He looked around her apartment and made for her tape recorder on the coffee table. "This. Is there a tape in here? Is it ready to use?"

"No. Well, I mean, there's a tape in there, but we used it."

"Do you have a new tape?"

She still couldn't read him. "What's this about, Nick?"

"Get the tape. There are questions you didn't ask me."

Startled, she came to a stop halfway to the closet where she kept her supplies. "What didn't I ask?"

He shook his head. "The tape."

She swore that if he came up with some lame question she was going to kill him. She didn't need him to fly halfway… *Oh, my goodness.* He'd flown halfway across the country. He'd come back to New York, the place he'd been adamant about never facing again. He wouldn't have done that for something trivial.

The hope inside her swelled and nearly burst out of every pore. She got the tape and inserted it for him.

"What am I supposed to ask?"

He took a long, slow breath. The muscles in his jaw flexed. "Here." He pulled a piece of paper from his pocket and unfolded it before handing it to her. He looked at the recorder in his hand for a moment, then pressed Record. "Read the first question."

Shannon looked at the list in her hand, but

her vision blurred. She had to blink several times to bring the words into focus. Then her heart thundered. "Mr.—" Her voice cracked. She cleared her throat and tried again. "Mr. Carlucci. When, if ever, are you returning to New York?"

"Well, Ms. Malloy, I'm back."

"Nick."

"This will work better if you stick to the list for now," he said, not meeting her gaze.

"Okay, sorry. It says, 'Oh, really? When did you get back?'"

"Just today as a matter of fact. My luggage is out in the hall. You see, I haven't found a place to stay yet. I wanted to get this interview finished first."

"Nick—"

He shot her a look.

Trembling in equal parts anticipation and

frustration, she looked at his list of questions again. "Mr. Carlucci, will you take a position with the FDNY?" *Oh, Nick.*

"As a matter of fact," he said, "I will."

"But you were adamant recently that you would never do it. What changed your mind?"

"The answer to that one's easy, Ms. Malloy." He pulled the list from her hand and let it drop to the floor. His dark eyes captured her gaze and held it, as his hands held hers. "I met a woman named Shannon. Just talking to her eased the darkness inside me and made me believe life was worth living. Not only that, she made me start to believe that I deserved to live and be happy. I happen to be in love with her and I'm hoping she'll give me a second chance."

Weeping with joy, Shannon threw herself into his arms.

Epilogue

Six Months Later
Tribute Park
Tribute, Texas

The big unveiling took place at 3:00 p.m. on a bright spring day. A new name had been added to the Tribute Wall. If the new bride had to practically hold a gun to her newly honored husband's thick head to get him to come back to town and let people fuss over him, well, he wasn't talking about it. They would just laugh at him.

But in spite of himself, Nick was humbled by the sight of his name on that wall. Shannon had done it. She'd gotten together with Bev and they had gone through whatever channels they'd had to in order to have his name added.

Nicholas Giovanni Carlucci
For uncommon bravery in saving several people from fire at the Tribute Inn by waking them in the middle of the night and even, in one instance, jumping through a wall of flames to reach Shannon Malloy and save her life.

"Congratulations, man." Fire Chief Lon Wallace slapped him on the back. "I know you don't like everybody making a fuss over you, but you know how it is. People gotta say thanks, you know?"

Nick sighed and shot his new wife a look. "Yeah, I know."

Half the town had turned out for the event. Schoolkids, teachers, parents. Some enterprising soul had even set up a refreshment stand over by the courthouse.

As Dixie and Wade said their goodbyes and everyone else wandered away, Shannon slipped her hand in his. "You did good today. I was proud of you."

"I can't believe you pulled this off completely behind my back."

She looped her arms around his neck and pressed a quick kiss to his chin. "I was desperate. I knew if you found out, you'd flip."

He studied the monument thoughtfully. "It's nice, you know? Having my name up there like that. I did something good, and somebody cared enough to tell people about it."

"There, see?" His wife of three months grinned at him. "You're my hero all over again."

He looked down into her eyes and knew he was the luckiest man alive. "I'll be your hero every chance I get. But I think your name should be up there in the hero column. You saved me, too, you know. If not for you, I never would have gone back to New York, I wouldn't be instructing at the academy and taking classes for arson investigation. So you're my hero, too."

"Oh, wow," she said softly, her eyes glowing. "Nick, you take my breath away."

"You took my fear away, and now you hold my heart. I love you."

Tears of joy trickled down her cheeks. "I love you, too."

* * * * *

β